"Cover my six," Trevor said, moving his chin in the direction of the shooter.

"Are you serious?" Sabrina asked. "If you go out there, you'll be an open target."

She wasn't wrong; there was little cover. "That's what you're here for," he said, smiling in an attempt to downplay the danger they were in and put her mind at ease. "You're going to have to put your money where your mouth is. You said you're a good marksman."

"I didn't mean I was *this* good. They have to be at least fifty yards away—way outside my comfort zone." She grabbed his hand, stopping him from moving. "Don't go." There was a deep well of concern in her eyes.

He had to act for the same reason she didn't want him to go—he had to shield her, the woman he loved.

Not that she could ever know that.

Though if she thought about it, she'd probably quickly realize that he wasn't the kind of man who would risk his life for just anyone.

Acknowledgments

This series wouldn't have been possible without a great team of people, including my #1k1hr friends, Jill Marsal and the editors at Harlequin—thank you for all your hard work.

Also, thank you to my readers. You keep me writing.

HIDDEN TRUTH

DANICA WINTERS

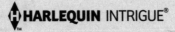

HARLEQUIN INTRIGUE®

To Mac, thank you for teaching me the meaning of true love.

ISBN-13: 978-1-335-60480-4

Hidden Truth

Copyright © 2019 by Danica Winters

Recycling programs for this product may not exist in your area.

www.Harlequin.com

Printed in U.S.A.

Danica Winters is a multiple award-winning, bestselling author who writes books that grip readers with their ability to drive emotion through suspense and occasionally a touch of magic. When she's not working, she can be found in the wilds of Montana, testing her patience while she tries to hone her skills at various crafts—quilting, pottery and painting are not her areas of expertise. She believes the cup is neither half-full nor half-empty, but it better be filled with wine. Visit her website at danicawinters.net.

Books by Danica Winters

Harlequin Intrigue

Stealth

Hidden Truth

Mystery Christmas

Ms. Calculation
Mr. Serious
Mr. Taken

Smoke and Ashes
Dust Up with the Detective
Wild Montana

Visit the Author Profile page at Harlequin.com.

CAST OF CHARACTERS

Trevor Martin—One heck of a bad boy and the dark horse of Mystery, Montana. When he moves to his family's ranch, the last thing he expects is to find himself knee-deep in a murder investigation with a woman who threatens everything he holds dear.

Sabrina Parker—The secretive and aloof woman hired to work as a housekeeper and general ranch hand, she quickly realizes she is falling for the man she can never have.

STEALTH—The Martins' private government contracting company, known for taking down those deemed unsavory by the US government and its many citizens.

Derek Mercer—The shady agent in charge who thinks everyone and everything belongs to him—even Sabrina, his employee and former flame.

Wyatt Fitzgerald—The local sheriff's deputy who quickly finds himself neck-deep in an investigation that calls into question not only his investigative skills but a whole slew of his community's history.

The Cussler Clan—The hillbilly family who lives at the back of the ranch; a family who has even more dark secrets than the Martins.

Chad Martin—Trevor's brother and the family clown. He takes very little seriously, but he is the man in the shadows who often controls far more than anyone expects.

Trish Martin—The youngest Martin sibling, who is killed in action during an undercover operation for STEALTH. Her death haunts the entire Martin family and leaves them all feeling broken and guilty.

Fenrisulfr Bayural—The leader of the Bozkurtlar, or the Gray Wolves, a terrorist organization that works around the globe and leaves only murder and mayhem in their wake.

Prologue

She clicked open the tabs of the gun case, exposing the M24 sniper rifle. It was a thing of beauty. Even without firing a single round from this particular gun, Trish Martin could recall the precise feel of pulling the trigger, smelling the spent powder and watching as her enemies fell to their knees.

There was no greater feeling in the world than a justified kill. The men standing around her, those dealing in death, would be easy to strip from this earth.

She ran her fingers down the synthetic stock, taking in the slight imperfections on the newly manufactured gun. This one would be for a different kind of kill, a long-term tactical assault, rather than a one-and-done straight to the head.

Some people were only too happy to judge her and her family for the work they did, but she didn't care. She didn't care that she was out there protecting the ones who didn't appreciate it right alongside the ones who did. She was a hunter, a predator, who fought for her territory and for life as she knew it.

The shroud of darkness wormed its way around her as she waited for the Bozkurtlar, or what some people called the Gray Wolves. To call them a Turkish crime syndicate was an understatement. No, they were so much more.

They were the reason she and her family were here in Adana, the reason she couldn't sleep at night, and the reason there were so many unmarked graves scattered around the Turkish hillsides. Their name suited them. No matter where in the world they were, death and mayhem followed.

That would all end soon.

She heard the sound of footsteps on the concrete floor and the clink of the metal door closing behind the group. From the sound, there had to be at least ten men. If anything went wrong…

She looked around her. They had made a mistake in agreeing to meet them in this shell of a warehouse. There weren't nearly enough hiding places or corners where she could find cover if she needed to. And there wasn't anywhere for her brothers to hide within the building. Without a doubt, the group's intention had been to isolate her and to strip her of any way to double-cross them.

"Ms. Stone," a man with a thick Turkish accent said from behind her. "I hope you aren't planning on brandishing that weapon. We're here to buy new, not used."

She stood up to face Fenrisulfr Bayural. He was nearly a foot shorter than her, but what he lacked in height, he made up for in his stance. When he stared at her, his golden-hued eyes took on the darkness that surrounded them, making her instinctively twitch for the gun at her side.

She stared down at him, forcing herself to act far more confident and self-assured than she felt in his presence. He couldn't sense weakness in her. If he did, he and the bodyguards around him would certainly pounce. When it came to running guns, buyers tended to get skittish.

Two years ago, in Egypt, one of her team's sting operations had ended with a shipment of American weapons falling into the wrong hands—and the men on her team being murdered. They were part of the reason she had ended up here—men, especially those with a Napoleon complex, tended to be more than happy to play nice with a hot brunette. But she'd be crazy to think her looks would keep this from becoming a firefight.

"We sell nothing but the best. You'd be a fool to think anything less," she said.

"Good. But will you also be providing more advanced weaponry or just the ARs?"

He wanted the launchers. Of course he did. But rocket launchers weren't something that they readily had on hand. Yet what he didn't know wouldn't hurt him. For now, she just had to play along and make it out of this room alive.

"How many did you want?"

"Four thousand RPGs and ten thousand ARs. I need my men to have adequate coverage when they attack Ankara."

As he spoke the name of the city, she felt the warmth of the mic strategically stitched into her jacket. They had their location and an estimated number of enemy combatants—admittedly, a number far greater than they had anticipated. But perhaps it was Bayural's plan to inflate the numbers. In the event any of their dealings leaked, he would appear far more powerful than he and his group really were.

"What do you have available for us?" Bayural crossed his arms over his chest, covering his vital bits as he prepared to negotiate his price.

No matter how he tried to protect himself, once her brothers bore down there would be no protection great enough. His life would be theirs for the taking.

"The Type 91 Kai MANPAD rocket launcher will do everything from annihilating a door to wiping almost an entire city block clean with its shoulder-launched surface-to-air missiles. They're easy to carry, cheap and fast to reload. Everything you want." She chuckled slightly as she realized how much she sounded like a used car salesman instead of a trained killer. Her mother would have been so proud.

Bayural squatted down and picked up the sniper rifle. He lifted it up as he stood and shifted the gun in his hands as though he was weighing it. "Hand me a round," he said, turning toward the guard to his right.

The man pulled a round from his pocket. Bayural jacked the round into the chamber, smiling at the metallic click and slide sound the gun made.

No. He couldn't be allowed to actually shoot the rifle. It would be too dangerous. They were here to keep the general public from falling into harm's way, not to place them into greater danger. "The gun is solid. The shipment will be solid. Our team, Black Dragon, will get them to you by tomorrow." She tried to sound nonchalant as she slipped in their fake name, the code word. Her team would be here any second to strike these bastards down.

Finally, they could cut off the wolf's head.

"Tomorrow? I want them within the hour." He lifted the rifle, pointing it directly at her center mass as he peered down the scope. "You can do that, can't you?"

She glanced toward the far wall, hoping like hell that she would see the laser signal letting her know her brothers were in place, but there was nothing.

"When can we expect your shipment?" Bayural pressed.

"First, I want my ten million."

Bayural smiled. "Ten is too much."

"With everything happening in Syria, prices have

gone up for your standard RPGs. You know as well as I do that the market is at least two Gs per RPG. As for the ARs, you are getting a screaming deal. That's less than two hundred a gun. We could get five if we went somewhere else."

He nodded slightly. "I'll give you a G per RPG."

She laughed. Even if she had really had the weapons, there would be no way she would go for such a ridiculous deal, but she had to keep up the negotiation until her brothers arrived.

"Or we will give you two if you can have our shipment to us within the hour." Bayural's pitch rose, like he was growing more nervous with each passing second.

His bodyguard leaned in and said something in his ear, something far too quiet for her to hear. Bayural's eyes widened and his brow furrowed. Whatever he said, it wasn't good news.

Her chest tightened, and her Kevlar vest suddenly seemed all too heavy.

Her brothers should have been here by now, at her side. "We can do the hour, but I'll have to talk to my team. Your order is larger than we were anticipating."

This was falling apart. Fast. She had to get out of there. She scanned the room for her planned exit point. The door to the alley was closed, barred from the inside. There was nothing to use as cover. It would take at least three seconds for her to get to the location, two to get the door open. Five seconds. Basically, a lifetime if they opened fire.

He clicked off the safety, the gun's barrel steady as it pointed at her. "Is something wrong, maybe you have something you want to tell us?" His voice threatening.

"No," she said, trying to appear relaxed as she took a step back. "But if you wish to have the deal go through, you need to lower that gun."

Bayural lowered the weapon slightly and motioned toward her with his chin. His guard took a step closer.

"What are you doing?" she asked as the guard grabbed her wrist and pulled her arm behind her. Her shoulder pinched as he lifted her hand higher, forcing her to submit.

Her instinct was to struggle and pull free, to launch into an attack. To get the hell out of there. But no, she had to trust her team. If they were waiting, there had to be a reason. They were trying to get more information. They must have needed more. She had to believe in her family.

"Back off," she growled at the guard. "Let go of my arm or the last thing you will see is me ripping it off and shoving it down your goddamned throat."

He lifted her wrist higher, forcing her to lean forward from the pressure.

"Bayural, get your man—"

"To stand down?" Bayural said, finishing her sentence. "Hardly. Who the hell do you think you are to command me?" He dropped the rifle to the ground and looked to his guard. "Break the stock."

She looked at the base where she had just run her fingers. The imperfection suddenly seemed so much larger.

The guard picked up the gun and smashed it against the floor again and again until cracks formed in the plastic. He batted it against the concrete one more time, sending the small GPS tracker her team had planted in the plastic skittering across the floor.

"You, your brothers, your sister, your team… You're dead."

"You may get me, but you'll never get the rest of them. We're survivors."

"Even if I have to spend the rest of my days on this earth hunting every one of your family members down, I'll do it. When I'm done, you and your kind won't even be a memory. You will be nothing."

There was a smatter of gunfire outside the corrugated steel building. A round pinged against the metal siding, the sound echoing through her.

With her free hand she reached down and pulled the knife from her boot. She jammed it deep into the guard's foot. The man screamed, letting go of her arm in a panic to remove the blade.

She grabbed her sidearm, taking aim at Bayural and pulling the trigger. The round ripped from the barrel, striking the man in the chest. Buyural didn't seem to notice the hit. He must have been wearing a vest.

The guards around him pulled their guns as she turned to find cover. Anything. Anywhere. She had to get the hell out of there. Now. She rushed toward the door as the sound of gunfire rained down upon her. The first round struck her in the thigh, ripping through her muscle with a searing heat, but there was no pain. Her ravaged thigh tripped her, the muscles failing to follow her brain's command. Her body fell to the floor, but she pressed on, dragging her injured leg behind her as she crawled toward the back door.

The door flew open, and standing in the nearly blinding light was her brother. "Trevor!" she screamed. "Get the hell out."

He ran toward her in what seemed like slow motion, but as he took two steps, the next round struck. Wetness. Warmth. Something had splattered her cheek.

She stopped struggling as she pressed her fingers to her face and traced the spatter to the gaping hole in her neck. No. This couldn't be real. This couldn't be happening. Not like this. Not now.

She sank to the floor as the blood poured from her.

The concrete was cold against her face as she watched the pool of red grow. The world narrowed to a pinpoint until all she saw was Trevor. His face. He'd

always been so handsome. So dangerously handsome. She'd miss her brother.

She'd miss them all.

Breathe. All she had to do was breathe. But as she
struggled to fill her lungs, there was only a strange
gurgling sound.

She had been wrong to think this operation would
be easy. Nothing in their lives had ever been simple. And now that misjudgment—and her desire to
trust—would prove fatal.

Chapter One

There was a single question that Trevor Martin hated above all others: "Who do you think you are?" It only ever meant one of two things—he was about to get slapped by a woman or he was going to have to knock some sucker out.

It wasn't the question that bothered him so much. On the surface it was just some retort people came up with when they didn't know what else to say, but when he heard it, he heard it for what it really was—a question of who he was at his core. And when he thought about that, about what made him the man he was, he wasn't sure that he liked the answer.

That self-hatred was one of the reasons he had taken a leave of absence from his contract work with the CIA. His entire family needed a break from the family business, so they bought the Widow Maker Ranch in Mystery, Montana. It was supposed to be an escape he so desperately needed from the thoughts of all he had done wrong in his life. Instead, it was as if the rural lifestyle and the quiet mountain mornings only made the self-denigration of his character that much louder.

He'd only been there a few days, but he couldn't help but wonder if maybe he'd made a mistake in coming to this forsaken place where he was constantly shrouded in clouds and imprisoned by the brooding mountains. Everything about the ranch made him long to stretch and push the world and his thoughts away—if only it were that goddamned easy. No matter where he went or what he did, his memories of the days he'd spent in his family's private security business, one they called STEALTH, constantly haunted him.

And here he was the bearer of bad news once again.

If he were being honest, pulling the trigger and tearing down an enemy combatant was a hell of a lot easier than what he was going to have to do. He spun the motorcycle around in the dirt, kicking up dust as he screwed around and tried to focus on something he loved instead of something he was going to hate.

After a few more doughnuts, he got off his Harley and pushed the kickstand into place with his foot. Taking off his helmet, he set it on the seat, though a part of him wondered if it wouldn't have been better for him to wear it as some kind of shield from the battle that was likely to ensue.

Running his hand over his too-long locks, he

pushed them out of his eyes and tucked them behind his ears.

There were times, just like this one, that he wished he were back in a war zone and had a staff of people under him who could handle this kind of thing.

All he had to do was say his piece, give them the letter, and he could get the hell out of there. He just had to go in and do his duty. The moment he and his brothers and his sister had purchased the land, they agreed that this would be a part of the work that would need to be done. Unfortunately, he had drawn the short straw.

He had never seen a picture of the house in question, but the shack in front of him was a squatter's paradise and far from what he and his family had imagined. The roof was a collection of corrugated steel in a jumble of different colors, and the siding, what was left of it, had started to rot and several pieces were only half-attached. Even the front door was cockeyed, listing to the left so far that there was at least a two-inch gap at the top.

Whoever resided there must be hard up. Maybe they had been hoping they were far enough out of the way at the farthest reaches of the ranch that they would go completely unnoticed. Thanks to the neglect of his cousins, the Johansens, whoever was living in this place had pretty much free rein—and their plan for disappearing in plain sight had worked.

And from the state of the house, it was clear it had been working for a long time.

The forest around the house was filled with junk, everything from antique wringer-style washing machines to the rusted-out shells of farming equipment. From the state of disrepair, it seemed likely that this had once been the dumping ground for the ranchers of years past.

He walked toward the door. Behind him a twig snapped and the sound was answered by the chatter of a pine squirrel high up in one of the trees.

He wasn't alone.

If he turned around now, it would give away that he was aware he was being watched. For all he knew, the inhabitants of the shanty had taken to the woods at the sound of his bike as he'd made his way down the makeshift road that led up to this place. If he just kept walking, it would give him time.

He started again, looking for a window or something he could use to catch a glimpse of whoever was lurking in the shadows around him.

They couldn't get the drop on him; he wouldn't allow it. He'd made it through years of toeing the line between danger and death, and he wasn't about to get tripped up and find himself on the losing side now. Not when he'd come here to make a real home and a real life for himself.

He stopped at the front door of the squatters' shack and started to knock.

"They're not home," a woman said from somewhere in the distance, her voice echoing off the timber stands around them and making the source of the sound impossible to pinpoint. "And they would have been long gone regardless, thanks to your crappy driving."

He turned in the direction the voice had come from and relaxed a bit. She probably wasn't going to try to shoot him—if she had wanted, she already could have drawn on him—but some habits died hard, and he lowered his hand to the gun that was always strapped on his thigh.

Standing in the shadows at twelve o'clock, her back against the buckskin-colored pine, was a blonde. She was leaning back, her arms over her chest like she had been there for hours getting bored. Even feigning boredom, she was sexy as hell. She had the kind of curves he had spent more than one lonely night dreaming about. And the way her white T-shirt pulled tight over her leopard-print bra… His body quivered to life as he tried to repress the desire that welled within him.

"You know where they went?" he asked, trying to be a gentleman and look at anything besides the little polka dots that were almost pulsing beneath her shirt.

She smiled as though she could see the battle that was raging inside him between lust and professional distance. "Have you met the Cussler boys before?"

"How many are there?"

She pushed herself off the tree. "If you stop thumbing that SIG Sauer at your side, maybe we can talk about it. Men playing with their guns make me nervous."

"You around men and guns a lot?" he asked, but the question was laced with a provocative tone he hadn't intended.

She walked toward him, and from the way she moved her hips even he, a man who had slept with only a handful of women, could tell that she had heard the inflection in his words as well…and she intended to do something about it.

He raised his hands in surrender. That's not what he'd come here for, not that he would have minded kissing those pink lips, not with the way they gently curved in a smile but hinted at something dangerous if they were allowed free rein. With the raising of his hands, she stopped and her smile faded. There was a small cleft in her chin, and damn if it didn't make her look even cuter than she had before.

Once, when he'd been young, his mother had told him, "Dimple in the chin, devil within." From the look in her eyes when she was staring at him and that damn bra she was wearing, there was plenty of devil within her.

"Are you Trevor?" she asked, not moving any closer.

He took a step back, surprised that the woman had any idea who he was. "Who are you?"

This time, she was the one to wave him off. "Your

brother hired me to keep house—starting here. He didn't tell me that I was going to need a backhoe and a dump truck."

Either she had accidently forgotten to supply him with her name, or there was a reason she was keeping it from him.

It hardly seemed fair she should know anything about him when this was the first he was hearing about her.

"You from around here?" he asked, motioning vaguely in the direction of Mystery in hopes she would loosen up with a little bit of small talk.

"Actually, I'm kinda new. Was looking for a slower pace of life."

"Well, it doesn't get a whole lot slower than here," he said, a darkness flecking his words. He hoped she didn't read anything into his tone. He didn't need to get into some deep discussion with a stranger about the merits or pitfalls of a place where he doubted he was going to stay.

"If you think it's slow in town then you haven't spent enough time in the mountains. These mountain men are about as fast as cold molasses and a little less intelligent. If you ask me, their family tree is more of a twig."

He laughed. "So where are you from…and hey, what's your name again?" he asked, trying to play it off like she had told him and he had simply failed to remember it.

She gave him an impish smile, and he could have

almost sworn that she fluttered her eyelashes at him. "Sabrina. And I'm from all over. Kind of an army brat, but my last stop was Schofield."

Instinctively, he glanced down at her arms. She was pale and far from the buttery color of someone who had spent their days in the Hawaiian sun. She had to be lying.

On the other hand, maybe he was reading far too much into her and her answer. Maybe she just valued her privacy like he valued his. Besides, if he was going to transfer into the civilian world, he would need to stop thinking everyone was out to conceal the truth from him—not everyone was his enemy, especially a housekeeper in the little town of Mystery, Montana.

But he'd been wrong before, and that failure to see danger had gotten his sister killed. He couldn't let his guard down. Not now. Not ever.

"Your father in the marines?" he asked.

"Schofield is an army base. I wouldn't make that mistake around a vet, if I were you." She sent him a dazzling smile.

She had passed the first test, yet something about her just didn't feel right—just like everything in his life since his sister Trish had died.

"How long have you been waiting on the Cussler boys?"

She shrugged. "I only got here a few minutes before you. To be honest, I was trying to figure out where to start the cleaning."

"So, they're gone?" His job of kicking the family out of their shanty was proving to be a whole lot easier than he had expected.

"They're not here, but I thought you had already come to kick them out. At least, that's what your brother led me to believe."

He was supposed to be here an hour ago, but he hadn't known his brother was sending a crew behind him or he would have been on it. "And you haven't seen any sign of activity?"

She shook her head. "But like I said, I only got here right before you."

He walked up to the door and knocked. There was the rattle of dishes as the mice, or whatever vermin it was that lived in the place, scurried over them. He went to knock again, though he was almost certain they were alone, but as he moved the door creaked open.

"Hello? Someone home?" he asked, walking in.

The place was dark and as he entered, a putrid smell wafted out—the brothers mustn't have been there in some time, or they were even worse at keeping house than they were at building one. He stepped in and the cobwebs in the corners of the front door clung to his face. He tried not to be squeamish as he wiped them away. No matter where he went in the world or what he was doing, he'd always hated that feeling. No amount of training or conditioning could get rid of the instinctual revulsion—and that was to say nothing of the inhabitants of the webs.

"Trevor," Sabrina said breathlessly from behind him. "Look."

He dropped his hands from his face and gazed into the dark shadows where she pointed. There, sitting against the corner, was a man. His face was bloated and his lips were the deep purple color of the long dead.

Trevor clicked on the flashlight on his cell phone and pointed it toward the man as he moved closer. Above his right ear, at the temple and just below the dead man's ruddy hair, was a small bullet hole. There was no exit wound on the other side. The man's eyes were open, but they had started to dry and shrink in the socket, in sharp contrast to the rest of the man's features.

"Do you see a gun anywhere?" Trevor asked, flashing the light around as he looked for the weapon that could have killed the man.

"No," she said, but she stood in the doorway staring at the man. She covered her mouth with the back of her hand as though she were going to be sick.

Trevor rushed over to her and wrapped his arm around her. "Come with me. Let's go back outside. It's going to be okay. You're all right. Everything is going to be fine."

She turned her body into him, letting him pull

her into his arms as he moved her out the door and to the fresh air of the forest. He had been right—she would be just fine; from the way she felt in his arms, he was the one who was truly in danger.

Chapter Two

Sabrina had no idea why she had reacted that way. The man was hardly the first dead body that she had come across, and yet it felt like the first time. Maybe it was the way he seemed to be looking at her through those cloudy eyes or the smell of the body that had been left sitting in the heat of the fall, but she just couldn't control her body's reaction.

Damn it. Every time she started to think that she was strong, she did something like this.

Although maybe it wasn't a bad thing that she had reacted as she had. She had gotten to play up the lady-in-distress angle. If she had to be undercover for any amount of time, it was going to be immensely easier if she had one of the brothers under her spell.

She just had to remember to keep him at arm's length; the last thing she needed to do was let her emotions come into play. Emotions only had a way of getting her into trouble, and she was in enough as it was. They were the reason she was stuck in this place…and out of the direct line of sight of her superiors. Though she was certainly under their thumb.

Trevor was just another case, another investigation she had yet to complete. In a month, if everything went according to plan, she would be out of here and set down in a new little nowhere town in the middle of America investigating another possible threat to homeland security.

Trevor rubbed her back and as he held her, his chest rose and fell so rhythmically that she found herself mimicking his movements. He was like a man version of a white noise machine, and just as soothing.

If she had to guess, between his dark brown hair, his crystalline blue eyes and a jawline that was so strong that it could probably cut glass, he was all women's kryptonite. He probably was the kind of man who had a woman every time he went downrange.

She pushed herself out of his arms and sucked in a long breath as she tried to completely dissociate herself from him. The last thing she needed was to share anything with him—even his breath.

"Are you feeling better?" he asked, looking at her like she was a bird with a broken wing.

She nodded. "I don't know what that was about. I'm sorry."

"That was about a dead man," he said, shock flecking his voice. "It's not something one sees every day. I would have been more worried if you hadn't reacted that way. Shock can be more dangerous than most flesh wounds."

Crap... She couldn't give herself away. Of course he would think she was a newbie to this kind of thing. She had to remember the role she had been sent here to play. A role that required that she be seen little and heard even less. What a joke for her superiors to play...they knew just as well as she did that silence wasn't her strong suit. She wasn't the kind of woman who was going to let anyone push her around, tell her what to do or require that she "let the men do the real work."

Her skin prickled at just the thought of the last time she had heard someone mansplain to her.

Trevor touched her arm. "Sabrina, you with me?"

"Huh? Yeah." She looked at him and forced a smile.

"Why don't you go and sit down," he said, pointing toward his motorcycle. "Or I guess you can lean." He gave her a guilty smile, realizing what an absurd idea that was.

"I'm fine. Do you think you should call the police?" She motioned toward the shack with her chin.

She would rather not have any local officers running around the place and mucking up her investigation or compromising her position.

Yet they couldn't hide a dead body...

Or could they?

If they swept this under the rug, it would give her more access to Trevor and his family without the threat of outside interference. It would definitely speed things up for her. If the police started poking around, the Martins would clam up and go even deeper into hiding.

And really, who would care about one mountain man who had turned up dead? He was totally off the grid, and as far as the government was concerned he was a nonentity. In fact, the only thing that his brothers, and folks like him, were known for were extremist ideals and a penchant for causing trouble.

Yet she couldn't be the one to bring up the idea of hiding the very dead Cussler brother.

Trevor stared in the direction of the shack. "We should call somebody…"

The way he spoke made her wonder if he was thinking along the same lines as her. No doubt, he didn't want anyone poking around, either.

"But?" she asked, prodding him on.

"I bet his family would go bonkers if we brought law enforcement out here. And the last thing this ranch needs is more craziness from the locals." He frowned. "We are just trying to fit in here. We don't want to draw unnecessary scrutiny from our new neighbors."

"Well, if you think that the Cusslers would appreciate us not—"

"Yes, I'm sure they would want to keep this a family issue." Trevor sounded sold on the idea.

She wanted to point out the possibility that the other members of the Cussler clan may be lying dead somewhere out in the timber as well. Otherwise wouldn't they have already buried their brother's body?

Yet she didn't want to press the issue. Not if it meant there was a possibility he would change his mind and call the police. Not that he would. She had the definite feeling he wanted to sweep this man's death under the rug just as much as she did.

"I'm going to go back in and take a look around," he said.

"Why?" she asked, before thinking.

He looked at her as though he was trying to decide how much he should open up to her. "If we're not going to call someone out here, we need to make sure that this isn't the work of some serial killer or something. You know what I mean?"

"You think he was murdered?" she asked, trying to play up the innocent and naive angle.

"My hope is that this is nothing more than a suicide. I just need to make sure."

She doubted that was really why he was going back in. He was probably looking for something more, something that would guarantee they wouldn't find themselves in deeper trouble if any of this ever came to light.

"You wait here. I'll be right back."

She grimaced. He hadn't really just tried to tell her what to do, had he? If he thought she was some kind of chattel that he could just order around, he had another think coming.

"Okay." She sighed as she tried to calmly remind herself he wasn't bossing her around out of some need for control; rather, it was his need to protect. "But be careful in there. If I know one thing about these kind of recluses, it's that they have a reputation for hating outsiders. They may have set up some kind of booby trap."

He stared at her like he was trying to figure her out. The look made her uncomfortable. "Got it, but I promise you have nothing to worry about when it comes to my safety. I have experience with this kind of thing."

His alleged role in peacekeeping and his family's Blackwater-type company was known, but she was surprised he was admitting any of it to her. Maybe her investigation wouldn't be as difficult as she had thought. Hell, if things went her way she could have all the answers she needed in a matter of days.

Then again, things would have to go her way, and life hadn't been playing nicely with her lately.

Trevor slipped back to the shack, holding up his phone as a flashlight as he made his way back inside.

She moved quietly after him. Maybe she could see something that he would miss, something that would prove the brother's death was nothing more than a suicide so they could put this all to rest.

As she walked toward the shack, she stopped. No. She couldn't pry. She couldn't get any more involved with this. If she went in there and did find something, there was a high probability that she would slip up and say something that would give away her background. He couldn't know anything about her position in the FBI.

She walked around to the back of the shack to where an old push lawn mower sat. There, on the ground beside it, was a puddle of dried blood. Pine needles had collected at the edges, making the pool look like some kind of macabre artwork.

She opened her mouth to call out to Trevor, but stopped. No. She couldn't tell him.

From the state of the body in the house, there was little possibility this blood belonged to the dead man. If someone had shot him out here and moved him, there would have been drag marks or some indication that the body had been staged. Though she hadn't spent long in the room with the dead man, she had noticed the blood leaking out of the wound at his temple. If she closed her eyes, she could still see the trail as it twisted down his ravaged features and leaked onto his dirty collar, staining it a ruddy brown. He couldn't have been moved postmortem. No, the blood pattern didn't match.

Which meant this blood had to belong to another

person. And based on the volume of it on the ground, they were possibly dealing with more than a single death.

Crap.

She stared at the dried blood. Kneeling down, she scooped up a handful of the sharp, dried pine needles that were scattered around. What she was about to do could end up going all kinds of ass-backwards, but it had to be done for her, for her investigation and for her chance at getting her future back. There was nothing she wanted more than to rise in the ranks, and sometimes that meant that sacrifices had to be made.

She threw the needles atop the blood and stepped onto them. She kicked away at the dried blood, earth and needles until there was nothing.

It felt wrong to destroy evidence, but at the same time a sensation of freedom filled her. It was refreshing to break the rules and to make her own in name of the greater good.

Walking around to the door of the shack, she poked her head inside. Trevor took a step deeper into the shadows around the dead body. He knelt down and moved aside a piece of discarded cloth on the floor. He chuckled.

As he stood up, she saw a gun in his hand. He wiped the grip and the barrel down with his shirt, as though he was stripping it of any possible fingerprints.

There was only one reason he'd wipe the gun

down—he was trying to protect the person who had pulled the trigger. Maybe that person was him.

Hell, he had probably come in here and killed the brothers in an attempt to get rid of them once and for all. Then he had waited for her to arrive before he rode up on his Harley like some kind of badass playboy.

He'd probably wanted her to see the man's body first. He'd wanted to come off as innocent. He'd wanted to take her in his arms and act the hero.

And she had allowed the bastard to set her up.

Chapter Three

Trevor walked up the front steps of the ranch house and waited as Sabrina parked her car and made her way over to him. He had told her that she could have the rest of the day off. She didn't need to come back to the main house with him—she could return to the old foreman's place, which was hers now—but she hadn't accepted his offer. Instead, she had only said that she had work to do.

Actually, it was the only thing she had said. The words had rung in his ears the entire ride back to the main house. There had been something in her sharp inflection that told him she was angry about something, something he was missing—and that there was danger afoot—but for the life of him, he didn't understand.

It was like he was married all over again, his life awash with unspoken anger and resentment. The memory of standing at the front door of his apartment, watching as his wife bedded another man on their once-pristine leather sofa, made a sickening knot rise in his belly.

Once again, just like before, he was forced to be an unwilling participant in things unspoken.

Hopefully this time he would be able to stop his life from falling to pieces in front of him.

She came to a stop beside him, but she was putting off a distinct "don't touch me" vibe.

He must have crossed some invisible barrier when he'd pulled her into his arms back at the shack, but it hadn't been his intention to make her feel uncomfortable. He had just been trying to help, to lend a shoulder to a woman in need, not to tick her off.

"Did you talk to Chad yet?" she said, glancing down at her watch like she was checking just how much time he'd had before she arrived.

He shook his head. Truth be told, he had been hoping she would keep driving instead of turning off on the little dirt road that led back to the ranch. It would have made sense, her running away after seeing the Cussler brother rotting in his chair.

And if she had kept driving, he could have had the real conversation he needed to have with Chad without worrying about what she would hear. Now he'd have to play it cool until he could get his brother alone and he had the chance to find out exactly what he knew. No doubt, Chad would have dealt with that man's remains as he had and left them out there for the Cussler family to handle.

They didn't need to draw undue attention. They needed to fly under the radar and off the grid for as long as possible.

He cringed at the thought of having to move again.

Getting out of Adana had been a nightmare after Trish's death. When they made their move to Montana, they sent misinformation on the dark net to make it seem like they were moving east to Thailand. They had no doubt that Turkish mobsters were just waiting for their chance to kill the rest of the family.

As long as nothing came out, they'd be safe for a while. It was the reason they had chosen this speck on the map. Plus, they'd have the cover of the United States and the amnesty that it offered if anything blew back on them. He and his family had done so many covert ops for the former president that they would always have government backup.

Or so he hoped.

Chad came sauntering out of the kitchen, a hot dog in his hand. He glanced from Sabrina to Trevor and gave him a raise of the brow as he stuffed the rest of the hot dog into his mouth, leaving a blob of mustard on his lip.

"I see you're already living the high life, brother," Trevor said with a laugh. "You want me to go in and get you a Budweiser, too? Nothing says American like a hot dog and a beer."

Chad swallowed the bite. "Not all of us developed a taste for world cuisine. You can't tell me that dolma is better than a good hot dog." He wiped off the speckle of mustard at the corner of his mouth with the back of his hand. "What do you think, Sabrina? You vote American food?"

She shrugged like she couldn't give a damn less. "Either, so long as I'm not cooking it."

"And that right there is the reason I hired you. I've always liked a woman who was as smart-mouthed as me. You are going to fit right in." Chad laughed. "Did you guys get the squatters handled?"

"Not exactly," Trevor said. He cocked his head toward Sabrina in a silent message to Chad.

Chad's smile disappeared. "Sabrina, do you mind getting started with your cleaning up here in the kitchen? 'Fraid I may have made a bit of a mess in there."

She opened her mouth to speak, but stopped and instead gave Trevor a look as though she hoped he would step in and allow her to take part in their conversation.

"Uh, actually…" Trevor stammered. "Sabrina, you must be pretty tired. Like I said, if you wanted to head back to your place—"

"No," she said, taking off her jacket and hanging it in the coat closet just inside the door. "I'll get started in the kitchen. I have a job to do, and this place isn't going to get any cleaner if I just go back to my place."

Sabrina strode into the kitchen and the door swung shut behind her.

"Let's step outside," Trevor said.

Chad followed him out and Trevor made sure to close the door behind his brother. He glanced in the front window of the house to make sure that Sabrina wasn't anywhere in sight. Thankfully, it looked as though she was in the kitchen.

"What in the hell were you thinking sending that woman out there?" Trevor asked, turning back to his brother. "Do you know what the hell I found in that shack? And because you were in some freaking hurry, Sabrina saw. Now she's a possible loose end."

"First, you were supposed to get out there long before her. You don't get to make this my fault. You should have stuck to the schedule."

"Had I known you were sending someone out behind me, I would have. How about you learn to freaking communicate?" Even as he said it, he couldn't help but feel that he was the pot calling the kettle black.

"What exactly did she see?" Chad asked, taking a step back from him like he was afraid that Trevor was going to take a swing.

"That damned Cussler guy was splattered all over the walls. Been dead at least two or three days." He pointed in the direction of the shanty. "I had to convince Sabrina that the dude was better off if we just left him and waited for the family to come back and collect his remains."

Chad turned around as he ran his hands down his

face. He stomped as he turned back. "Are you kidding me? We haven't been here a week and there's already a dead bastard in our back forty?"

"You should have just left me to handle my end of things, man. I had this taken care of. All I needed was a little time. But no, you wanted to rush things. To make sure everything was cleaned out and taken care of before Zoey and Jarrod arrive."

"You know how they can be—they were even more adamant than I was about the absolute need for privacy here. This family is all we have, Trevor."

"You don't need to tell *me* that."

Chad took in a long breath as though he were trying to collect himself. "So, was the guy's death a suicide or what?"

"There's no goddamned way. Someone shot him." He thought of the handgun he'd left sitting on the ground beside the dead man. "The gun was too far away from the body. No major stippling around the entrance wound, and the bullet had lost enough velocity that it didn't even travel through the entire skull—there was no exit wound. I'm guessing whoever pulled the trigger had to be at least ten to fifteen feet away."

"And where did you say you found the man?"

"He was sitting up in a chair, like someone got the drop on him. He didn't even have time to stand. He didn't see it coming."

"What about the rest of the hillbilly clan…did you find them? They alive or dead?"

"Hell if I know." Trevor threw his hands into the air. "I'm hoping that they just ran off. We don't need a dead family on our hands."

"Did you get a chance to look around?" Chad asked. "Wait, did you and Sabrina call in the locals?"

Finally, Chad was beginning to understand the implications of his screwup. If only he hadn't been in a hurry, they wouldn't already be compromised.

"Sabrina went along with keeping it quiet, but I don't know how long she'll be up for maintaining that." He glanced back inside, but the beautiful and stubborn woman was nowhere in sight. "She hasn't been acting right, ever since…" *I held her in my arms.* He didn't finish his thought.

"Huh? Ever since what?" Chad pressed.

"Since she saw the body. I'm afraid she may be a liability."

"What are you saying?" Chad asked. "You think she needs to disappear?"

"No," Trevor said, almost the same moment his brother had uttered the question. "No. We can't harm her. She hasn't done anything wrong. And who knows, maybe I made a mistake in thinking she can't be trusted. Maybe she won't be a problem."

Chad shook his head. "What if she does tell some-one? What if it comes out that we tried to cover up a man's death at our new ranch?"

Trevor stared at his boots. "She wouldn't…"

"Dude, if she tells anyone… First, we are going to look as guilty as hell. Second, our faces are going to be spread across the world in a matter of hours."

"She won't say anything."

"And how are you going to know if she does or doesn't? For all we know, she's in there texting her mother's brother's cousin about what you guys found. Hell, she could be sending pictures of the dead guy." Chad paused. "You know that I don't want to hurt an innocent woman. Not after what happened in Turkey… And Trish…" Their sister's name fell off his brother's tongue like it was some secret code, some unspoken link between past and present.

"Then let's leave her be."

Chad shook his head. "No. If you don't want to neutralize the threat, you're going to have to watch her like a hawk. Every move she makes, you need to be there… hovering."

"And what about the squatters? The body?"

Chad sighed. "What about it? Like you said, let that guy's family handle it."

"And what if they do, and they call the police?"

"If they haven't already, they aren't about to now." Chad stared at him. "For all we know, one of them is the one who pulled the trigger—or else they're lying out there in the woods somewhere, too. Either those bastards are on the run or they aren't going to be spilling any secrets any time soon."

"Do you think I should go back out there? See if I can find them? Make sure that they're going to stay quiet?"

Chad stared out in the direction of the main pasture, but Trevor could tell that he wasn't really looking at anything. "I'll talk to Zoey and see if we can find out a little more on these Cussler guys. I want to know how many hillbillies were living out there, and who would have wanted them dead. I want to make sure that whoever is responsible for pulling that trigger isn't about to bear down on us."

His brother was right. They needed to make sure they weren't about to be ambushed.

"Most importantly," Chad continued, "I want you to keep Sabrina quiet. If you don't…you know what's at stake."

"She won't be a problem." Trevor paused, thumbing the gun at his side and letting it comfort him from his barrage of thoughts. "Hey…you don't think these Cussler guys have anything to do with STEALTH, do you?"

Chad shook his head, but from the way his face pinched, Trevor could tell that he was wondering the same thing. "Bayural and the Gray Wolves couldn't know that we are here. Zoey has made it her business to make sure of it. Everything we did has been in cash, or through Bitcoin. We're covered."

"Just because our sister is a computer whiz, it doesn't mean that we are safe. You know how easy it is to find someone, especially a group like our family. One stupid random selfie with us in the background and we're in danger. They are using the same facial recognition software that we are."

"Zoey has this under control," Trevor said, trying to give them both a little comfort—it had always been his job to keep the peace within the family, a job that had proven harder than ever thanks to his failure with Trish. His mistake was something that neither he nor the rest of his siblings would ever forget. "Besides, Zoey has made it her personal mission to keep them chasing fake hits around the globe. From what she said this morning, she currently has us pinging at a marketplace in Cairo."

Chad chuckled. "God, can you imagine those bastards' faces when they realize that they've been set up? I would almost pay to see it."

There was the clatter of pans hitting the floor from inside the kitchen.

Chad bounded up the porch steps and cracked the door. "Sabrina, you okay in there?"

"Fine, just fine!" she called back, sounding harried.

"Where did you find this woman?" Trevor asked, motioning toward the house.

"She came recommended from Gwen when we bought the ranch. They hired her when they were getting the ranch ready for us to take it over."

"So, just because our cousin—whom we barely

know—thinks this woman is trustworthy, you took her word for it?" Trevor was surprised. Chad wasn't one for details but he was normally careful about who they brought into their lives.

"Brotato chip, you seriously have to pull the stick out of your ass. You're starting to act like Jarrod."

He was nothing like their oldest brother. Jarrod had been a lone wolf since the moment he called upon them to take their positions within the business. After he had set up STEALTH he hit the road, looking for assignments from various governments.

"I hope Zoey looked into her background," Trevor pressed.

"Of course. Zoey said she was clean, nothing too much to tell. Looks like Sabrina had been travelling around the world with her military family until she turned eighteen, just working odds-and-ends jobs since then."

It was in line with the little Sabrina had told him, but something still felt wrong. Trevor glanced toward the kitchen where Sabrina was working. Maybe someday, if he could just ease himself back into being a civilian, something might start feeling right.

A man could only hope.

Chapter Four

She sat in the corner of the barn, letting the streak of morning sun that was leaking through the siding spread over the tips of her boots. Though the beam had to be warm, she couldn't feel it through the leather. Maybe the sun was just like the rest of her life...pretty to look at, but completely devoid of feeling.

Then again, yesterday had been full of them— at least when it came to Trevor. She glanced down at her phone and his picture. The photo was sharp, black-and-white, typical of the FBI. And yet it didn't really capture the man she had met. No, in real life he was far less imposing than he seemed in the picture. The photo failed to show the way it felt to stand there encircled in his arms, and then to realize that he had been playing her from the moment they met.

She flipped to the email from her handler, Agent Mike Couer, and stared at the man's instructions. She'd have to play nice, get along and then get out of there. If she didn't screw this up, she could be in and out without the Martins even knowing who she was or what she did. She'd made it this far; as long as she didn't get wrapped up in another set of arms, she'd be just fine.

For a moment she considered calling Mike and telling him about the body they had found, but she stopped. There wasn't enough evidence to track this back to the family. Sure, she could probably take Trevor down for the murder, but that wasn't what she was here for; no, she was here for them all. They had to be stopped before they put any more weapons into the hands of terrorist organizations…and that was to say nothing of the lives that they themselves had snuffed out. This family was likely responsible for the deaths of thousands of people, if not tens of thousands.

The thought made the anger bubble up inside her. These days that feeling, that fire, was her only constant companion. Without it, she wouldn't know who she was. It was that feeling that propelled her forward, past the crap in her personal life, and helped her to focus on her prime objectives. Her life wasn't hers to live. Her life belonged to the people of the world, people who deserved to be kept safe and out of the line of fire of the Martins.

Stuffing the phone back into her pocket, she made her way into the house.

She just needed to get her hands on as much information about the incident in Turkey as possible. There were reports of photos, pictures proving that the STEALTH team had been involved in the illegal gun trade, and during the event civilians had been shot and killed. If she could just prove it, or find evidence that the family was part of organized crime, not only would her past indiscretions at the agency be forgiven, but she might also find her way out of the remote offices and back to DC.

The house was silent as she weaved between the moving boxes. Trevor and Chad had been vague in their plans for the day, but she expected nothing less. No doubt, they were at the shanty taking care of their mess. She should have been out there with them, getting information about their possible involvement with the dead man and his family, but she hadn't found a way to get herself invited along. And really, even if she caught Trevor red-handed with this murder, where would it get her?

He was good at keeping people in the dark, but his family wasn't as good as they thought they were. She'd get what she needed. She always did.

Trevor's bedroom door was closed, but his room seemed like as good a spot as any to start. She opened the door. The room had nothing but four boxes, a desk, and a mattress and box spring on the floor. At the head of the bed, there was a rolled-up mummy bag sitting on a large body pillow.

Apparently, even though he had nothing, he was a man who still liked to make his bed in the morning.

Grabbing a box, she set it on the bed and pulled off the tape. As it opened, the scent of sand and sweat rose up and met her—the smell of war.

Well, she could fight, too.

She pulled out a set of fatigues. They were green and brown, a throwback to what Americans once wore in the jungles of Vietnam—not what she would have expected from desert warfare. The last time she'd seen an operative wearing this was in northern Africa. Some of the insurgents there loved to use the fatigues almost as their own personal calling card. They had even taken to calling themselves al-Akhdar, or "the Greens."

It didn't surprise her that this man would have found himself alongside such an infamous group. From what little she knew about them, the Martins had a way of being in prospective war zones even before the leaders of the country knew they were under fire.

She lifted the uniform out of the box and hung it up in Trevor's closet. Though she never had time to clean her own apartment back in Washington, coming in undercover as a cleaning lady had its benefits. She could almost openly go through whatever she wanted under the guise of her newfound job.

It didn't take long to empty the box and move to the next, putting away things as she came across them. Though she hadn't expected to find much in the boxes, she had hoped that maybe he'd tucked something away—a picture, some sentimental token—but there was nothing. In fact, aside from his picture and the few boxes that were in the room, there was little to prove that this man truly even existed.

The only things she'd been able to glean so far, thanks to what she'd managed to overhear from the brothers this morning, was that the rest of the family—Zoey and Jarrod—would be arriving sometime soon. When they got there, she would have little time alone in the house. She'd have to work fast.

After going through what amounted to four boxes of random clothing and a set of encyclopedias that she was sure dated from the 1980s, she folded up the boxes. Carrying them under her arm, she stepped toward the door. As she moved, she noticed a gap between the head of the bed and the wall. It wasn't much, just a couple of inches.

Making her way over to the gap, she pulled back his pillow, exposing a long black gun case.

Now we're talking.

She pulled out the case, gingerly setting it on the bed and clicking open the tabs. In the belly of the case sat an M107 .50 caliber. She'd only seen a few of these in her days, and they were always in the hands of snipers—army snipers, to be exact. She snapped a quick picture of the gun and its serial number, but made sure not to touch the weapon. She sent a quick message to her people at the Bureau, hoping that one of them could pull up something.

He had played her when he'd brought up Schofield. He must have been testing her. Which meant there had been something about her that made him think that she couldn't be trusted. Or maybe he mistrusted everyone. She racked her brain trying to think of something she had said or done that could have blown her cover, but nothing came to mind. She'd played it pretty cool...except for the girlie bit.

Or perhaps he wasn't Army after all. If his family had in fact been running weapons, as they assumed, then maybe this was just one from their catalog. There was little reason for Trevor to have such a specialized weapon out here in the Middle of Nowhere, Montana. Unless he feared for their safety, or he thought he was one phone call away from having to kill someone.

She was probably right in assuming he was the type who was always looking over his shoulder. It probably came with his kind of game.

Maybe it was that she simply saw some of her own life mirrored in his. Over the last year, thanks to her little slipup—okay, major setback—she had been away from home and the Bureau nearly the entire time. In fact, there had been only three days that she was in the office. One when she went in to see *him*, one when she was called into her superior's office and told she would henceforth be working remotely, and then when she was packing up her desk. Ever since then, she'd been living out of hotel rooms around the world. Everything in her life had been temporary and single-use.

She ran her fingers through her smooth hair. Since she'd taken residence at the Widow Maker Ranch she'd finally gotten the chance to buy and use real shampoo again, and not be stuck with the cheap stuff that was always in the guest basket at the hotels where she stayed.

Compared to Trevor's constantly on-guard life—a life that required high-caliber rifles and owning nothing but a smattering of dusty old clothes—a few split ends seemed to pale in comparison. At least she had a certain amount of freedom. For the most part, she could check out when she was off duty.

For a split second, she felt a niggle of pity for the handsome Trevor Martin. He was never going to be able to live a normal life, not doing what his family did. They would always be hunted. And forget about having a love life.

The pity turned to something else, something entirely too much like disappointment.

She was just being silly. What was going on with her since she met this man? It was like she had never been around a good-looking, dangerous, Harley-riding, perfectly built badass before.

She closed the gun case, slipping it back in exactly the same position she had found it.

No doubt with her unpacking his room and all, he would probably assume she had seen it, but she didn't want to make it blatant. And hopefully he would brush it aside, thinking she was the kind of woman who knew nothing about guns.

Her secret made a smile flutter over her lips. There was just something thrilling about being something and someone that no one expected at first glance. It was almost like a superpower...if she were a superhero, she'd have a cool name. No, better than cool—she'd want something enigmatic, mysterious. Something like the Shadow Defender, keeper of secrets and protector of the innocent.

She giggled as she walked out of the room, running smack-dab into Chad. Looking up, she tried to cover the guilt that was no doubt marking her features. Damn it, how had he gotten in without her hearing anything?

"Hey," she said, stepping around him. "I thought you guys were out for the day."

Chad glanced toward his brother's room. "Uh, yeah. What were you doing in there? Does Trevor know you were planning on going in there?"

She gave him her most alluring smile, hoping that she could bring down his suspicions in true female superhero style. "I just thought I'd get a move on unpacking all the boxes. I was going to go ahead and hit your room next. That way you guys have a comfortable safe haven to come home to at the end of the day." She shifted her weight, subtly exaggerating the curve of her hips. "There's nothing worse than a barren room."

Chad's eyebrow rose.

Crap, hopefully he didn't think she was making a move on him; she hadn't meant anything. No, not when it came to him. Chad was good-looking enough, but he wasn't nearly as handsome as Trevor. She thought back to the way Trevor had taken off his helmet and swept the long hair from his eyes. If he had a fan blowing on him, she might as well have been watching a freaking modeling shoot.

She turned before Chad could get any clue as to what she was thinking. The last thing she really needed was either brother assuming there was any possibility of something more than an employee-employer situation.

"Sabrina?" Chad called after her. "If you don't mind, I'll go ahead and unpack my things. No need for you to worry about it."

She waved behind her, not bothering to look back. There went her chance, at least for now, to get into his room. At least she had a starting point to her investigation. If she ran the serial number on the .50cal, maybe she could pull up something. If she was lucky, there would be some agency out there tracking the gun, but based on what had just happened, luck wasn't on her side.

She made her way to the newly remodeled kitchen, which still smelled of paint. As she pulled a box of Cap'n Crunch out of the pantry, the back door opened and Trevor strode in. He was sweaty and shirtless, wearing only a pair of running shorts and tennis shoes. He stopped and stared at her for a moment too long before he shut the door. Apparently he hadn't been planning on bumping into her, either.

He wiped his forehead with the back of his hand as he walked over to the cupboard by the sink and grabbed a glass of water. Since his back was to her, she could make out a droplet of sweat slowly twisting down the thick muscles along the tanned skin of his spine. The bead moved slowly, making her wonder if it tickled.

"I see you're one for a healthy start to the day. I like it," he said, filling up his glass and turning around with a cheesy, oh-so-cute smile on his face.

"The Cap'n and I have a long-term relationship," she said, hugging the box to her chest like it was a bulletproof vest. "He knows just how to make me smile."

"I hear you. I'm a sucker when it comes to food."

"You know what they say about the way to a man's heart," Sabrina said, but as the words escaped her, she just as quickly wished she could rein them back in.

Why couldn't she just be normal around this guy—flirty, yet out-of-bounds? Instead, here she was saying things that she couldn't have imagined herself saying when she was forced to take this assignment.

"In that case," Trevor said, grabbing a towel and dabbing at his forehead, "would you mind pouring me a bowl? I'll be right back, just going to go put on a shirt." He flipped the kitchen towel over his shoulder.

Hold up, had he really just implied she could make her way into his heart? No. He couldn't have meant anything like that.

As he walked away she once again found herself staring at the little bead of sweat, which now sat at the subtle indent that marked the place where his hips met his back. Her gaze moved lower as he walked away. His shorts moved in perfect harmony with his round, toned behind.

Yeah, she could touch that. Chances were, he would fit perfectly in the cup of her hand.

Wait, he was playing her. She couldn't fall for his abundant charms or his easy grace. No.

She turned around and grabbed a bowl from the cupboard and poured him some cereal, carefully setting the milk on the table beside it so he could add it in when he came back.

Her phone pinged with an email. Checking around her to make sure no one was near before opening it, she unlocked her phone. There was a message from

Mike. Just seeing his name pop up on her screen made her stomach clench. Just once, she would have liked to not have that feeling. It was stupid, really. His name would always pop up. He was too involved in her life for him to just disappear. If anything, she was foolish to think she would just get over him and be able to go back to work and pretend that nothing had happened between them.

Maybe she would have been better off quitting her job and moving on to something else, but she had told herself she was a big girl—able to handle anything that life threw at her, that she would just have to accept the consequences that came with her choices… and yet she seemed to always die just a little every time she saw anything to do with her former flame.

She hated him. Everything emotional he represented. He was the embodiment of all of her worst flaws—her inability to say no, to make people unhappy, and the weakness she felt when it came to the needs of her heart. If only she could turn the damned thing off, be cold, distant, professional.

Opening the email, she read the encrypted note:

Dear Ms. Parker,

In regard to your findings at your current posting, we are and have been aware of your assignments' past—including jobs dealing with long-gun usage. I'm glad to see you are finally making headway. Too bad it has taken you this long.

If you fail to meet the goals and standards set forth in your proposal in a timely manner, the SAC has let me know that they will be forced to look elsewhere for a UC who is better qualified. You have a week.

—M.C.

What a bastard. Mike had known what Trevor was and he'd left it out of the case files he'd handed her. He was trying to get her fired.

Of course.

What had she been thinking, assuming her sentence would be simple banishment to a remote office as an undercover agent along with her former flame? The special agent in charge, or SAC, whom they'd been forced to report to regarding their relationship had put them together out here in the middle of nowhere, hoping that they would learn to get along and develop a new sense of trust with each other. But the move had been ill-advised. As it was, she had a feeling she was in a dog-eat-dog battle with her ex, and only one would leave this kennel alive.

No big deal. She could do this. In fact, there was no better impetus for her to kick butt and take names than someone thinking she was incapable—or, in this case, Mike thinking he had the upper hand and assuming he could get rid of her that easily. She would show him, and the rest of the Bureau, exactly what she was made of.

The door to the kitchen opened and Trevor walked in. His smile had disappeared.

"Were you looking for something in particular?" he asked, the playful edge in his voice completely gone.

"Excuse me?" she asked, feeling the blood rush from her face as she stuffed her phone in her pocket.

"You went through my things. Why?" he said, staring at her.

She paused, thinking about every syllable before she spoke. "Your family hired me to do a job. I am here to help you get this house in order." She walked to the drawer and pulled out a spoon for him and set it down on the table beside his bowl like it was some kind of olive branch. "I have no interest in disrupting your life or invading your privacy," she lied, forcing her face to remain unpassable.

"Then why?"

"I told you why. I want to help." She sat down at the table, hoping he would recognize her contrition. "Look, I understand you're nervous. But about the man we found yesterday…"

Some of the anger disappeared from his face. "Did you tell anyone about the body?"

She shook her head. "Like I said, I am here to make your life easier, not cause more problems. If you don't want me to go in your room anymore, I won't." There wasn't anything in there she was looking for anyway.

He sighed. "No, don't worry about it. I guess I'm just a little jumpy. I'm not used to civilian life."

"That's okay. We're just going to need to start learning to communicate a little better with each other—especially when it comes to our boundaries." She motioned for him to sit.

He picked up the spoon as he sat down, finally a bit more relaxed in her presence.

Maybe she wasn't so bad as a UC after all—given time, she would get exactly what she needed.

Chapter Five

Trevor didn't quite know what to make of her. On one hand, Sabrina seemed to be everything a cleaning woman would be—focused, driven and into all of his things. On the other hand, the mere thought of someone poking around his house made him clench. He hadn't had a woman taking care of his life for him since…well, he was a child.

Done with breakfast, he walked back to his room. He hadn't had a closet, at least one that wasn't in a hotel or rented room, in forever. It was strange to think he actually owned something. In a way, it felt like a leash tying him to this place.

He had spent entirely too much time being out in the world and on his own to adjust to this kind of lifestyle overnight, but he had to admit that it would be nice to just hand things over to someone else for a while. For once, he could just focus on living.

A pit formed in his stomach. He'd been working in the shadows for so long he wasn't quite sure what living actually meant. The only thing he knew for sure was that he didn't want to be alone.

He thought of the way Sabrina had looked over breakfast, her long hair falling down in her face like gentle fingers that longed to caress her cheeks. He'd wanted to reach over and brush the tendrils out of her face, but as much as he had desired it, to touch her seemed wrong…especially after what had happened at the Cusslers'.

No matter how beautiful she was, she was clearly not interested in him. And yet if there was one reason he was glad to be leashed to this place, it was because of her.

But could he trust her?

He closed his bedroom door and walked to the head of the bed. Lifting out the gun case, he looked at the latch. The hair he'd left tucked in the lock was gone. She'd seen his gun.

No wonder she had been so strange with him, nervous even. He could only guess what she thought of him. Hopefully she thought he was just some redneck with a penchant for high-end weaponry. Or better yet, she hadn't a clue what she was looking at.

He pulled a hair from his head and put it back in the latch, setting the booby trap again. If she came back…well, they were going to have to have a longer talk. He'd show her exactly how well he could communicate.

Slipping the gun case back, he sat down on his

bed and pulled out his phone. Zoey had sworn that she'd looked into the woman's background, and he trusted his sister's judgment and aptitude when it came to technology…and yet, every cell in his body was telling him that Sabrina wasn't all she seemed to be. Zoey had to be missing something. He didn't know much about housekeepers, but it couldn't have been normal for them to open a gun case…that was, unless they were going to strip it down and clean the gun, or if they were looking for something.

Whatever she was looking for, she wasn't going to find it in his gun case. The only thing she'd find there was a recipe for disaster.

He unlocked his phone and went to his secondary email. Ever so carefully, he wrote:

Dear Ahmal,
My team will be in place Wednesday night for the handoff. Johnson and Beckwith. City Centre. Seven o'clock.
T

If Sabrina was a spy, she'd have it read within the hour. If she was a decent spy, she'd have men in downtown Seattle Wednesday at seven.

He emailed Zoey using his private server, letting her know to keep eyes on the fake drop.

The pit that had formed in his stomach started

to dissipate. For now, he'd done all he could to put his mind at ease…at least when it came to Sabrina.

He still needed to get to the bottom of the Cussler murder.

Crap. What if she is tied to the murder?

No. He shook his head at the very thought. She was suspicious, but she didn't seem like the type who would kill people. He'd seen those types more than he could count, and she didn't carry the same darkness in her eyes.

If anything, her blue eyes were like the sky… open, bright, and full of promise. And the way she sometimes looked at him, when she was unguarded it was like she wanted…well, she wanted *him*.

Yep, he was definitely losing his edge.

He needed to get to work.

As he made his way from his room and the traps he secretly hoped she wouldn't step into, Sabrina was whisking her way around the living room, dusting.

"I need to head up to check out the Cusslers. You wanna go with me?" he asked, trying not to notice the way her jeans hugged her curves as she bent over to dust the bottom of the built-in bookcase next to the television.

"Sure." She turned and smiled. "I don't know if you know this, but there is only so much of a mess that a man and his brother can make in a house. I swear, I've dusted this room at least three times in the last day. I could use a break."

He chuckled. "I can't say that I've dusted three times in my entire life. What's the point? It's just going to get dusty again."

She laughed, the sound high and full of life, and it made his longing for her intensify. It would have been so easy to take her back into his arms. She was…incredible.

Maybe being around her today was a mistake, not only professionally but personally as well.

"I…" he started, but the sound came out hoarse and he was forced to clear his throat. "Sorry. I was just going to say, I was thinking about running over to see our cousin at her family's ranch, Dunrovin. Maybe we could borrow a couple of horses and ride around the property and maybe a bit up the mountains behind the squatters' place…see if we find evidence that could help us get to the bottom of this guy's death."

Her face pinched for a moment, but then her smile returned…this time not quite reaching her eyes. "I haven't been on a horse in years, but I'd be happy to help you out. Investigating a murder is far more fun than cleaning a house." She walked to the coat closet and grabbed a jacket before turning back to him. "Wait, should I not say that? You being my employer and all?" She gave him a melting smile.

It worked.

"I'm not your employer…that would be my brother." He took her jacket from her and lifted it so she could simply slip her arms into it. As she moved under his hands, his fingers grazed her skin, sending sparks shooting through him.

He tried to ignore the way she made him feel, but the more he ignored it the hotter the sparks seemed to burn.

He walked a few steps behind her on the way out to his motorcycle. For a moment, she stood staring at it. "Um, do you just want to take my car?"

He checked his laugh. "What? Are you afraid of a little danger?"

Sabrina gave him a cute little half smirk. "There is a difference between danger and a death wish. Do you know how many people die each year on these things?"

Though he couldn't deny her logic, she wasn't seeing the bigger picture. "I've always thought life should be lived to its fullest. Sure, you can stay in a safe little bubble and live an extra day, or you can grab life by the horns and ride it for all it's got."

She laughed. "Of course, you would say that…if you want to ride, feel free, but I'll be following you in my car."

In a strange way, he found comfort in her refusal. Clearly, she wasn't the kind of woman who sought an adrenaline rush…or who wanted to court danger. Rather, she seemed to want to play by the rules. No one who lied for a living played by the rules all the time. There was a certain level of gray that just came with the life. He couldn't count the number of times he had been forced to break the law in order to serve the greater good. It was one of the things he had missed most about standing in the countryside of Turkey, running guns over militarized borders and taking down men who deserved to die a thousand painful deaths in recompense for the horrendous crimes they had committed.

Trevor had always considered himself to be on the side of righteousness when he'd been in the thick of things, but now…looking back, he couldn't help but wonder if he had made mistakes. There had been plenty of times when he didn't have to pull the trigger, when he could have let his target go…and yet, he'd never flinched. For him, there was never any hesitation. He was just there to do his job, do right by his family and get home safely. He'd never questioned his orders or his assignments. But what if he should have? What if he had killed innocents?

"Let's go ahead and take your car. I don't have a helmet for you anyway. And the last thing I'd want is for you to get hurt." He motioned toward her beat-up Pontiac. The paint was chipping around the wheel wells, and what paint remained was bubbling with rust. Clearly not a Bucar—a Bureau car—so she couldn't have been sent here by the Feds. That was, unless they had put her in this junker so she wouldn't fall under any unwanted scrutiny.

They did undercover well, but they weren't this good.

Besides, what could he possibly be under investigation for—they worked for the CIA. However, in the US government, they were notorious for the right hand not knowing what the left hand was doing…and it had only gotten worse with the new leadership in the Oval Office on down.

Then again, she could have been working for a foreign government. The Gray Wolves were known to have people planted throughout the Turkish government, and he wouldn't have doubted that they also had government allies in and around Europe.

He sighed as he opened her door and helped her into the car. He was making something out of nothing. Though he wasn't completely innocent, he wasn't guilty, either. He just needed to relax.

He walked around to the passenger side and stopped for a moment, trying to contain the writhing ball of snakes that were his feelings. Even if an innocent person had been killed, it hadn't likely been by him. He'd only fired on his enemies, but…they had been in an enclosed space. What if a round had ripped through the building and somehow struck someone outside? It had been known to happen.

In his time in the military, they'd touched on the topic of collateral damage time and time again. He'd always told himself that he was above making mistakes, especially ones that involved lives… but now he couldn't help questioning himself.

He'd let his sister down. He'd let her die. What if he'd killed someone else's family member in the process?

He closed his eyes, but the second he closed them he saw Trish's face, looking up at him as the pool of blood around her grew. He'd tried to save her. He'd killed at least five men getting to her, but by the time he'd gotten her to safety, it was already too late.

Every night since he'd gotten back to the States, he'd had the same nightmare—him doing those damned chest compressions on Trish. Waiting for her to take a breath. Checking her pulse. And watching in terror as he realized she was gone.

He was living in his own personal version of hell.

He'd never forgive himself.

All he could do now was protect the family he had left. And that started with making sure this Cussler guy's family wasn't going to come after them or bring the law down on them. They didn't need any more trouble.

As they drove to Dunrovin, he caught himself glancing over at Sabrina again and again. She seemed to be concentrating entirely too hard on her driving. Her eyes were picking up the light as it streamed in through the windshield, making them look even brighter. And now, in the sun, he could see the fine lines around her eyes and at the upturned corners of her mouth—the lines of someone who loved to laugh. In a way, it made her seem even more beautiful. Whoever had her on his arm was a lucky man.

"Have you been to this place before?" he asked, forcing himself to look away.

She nodded. "Yeah, I helped Gwen move their stuff to the new place when she and her mother decided to sell you all the ranch. Dunrovin is really nice. They've had some trouble in their past, but now they are up and running and doing well as a guest ranch."

They must not have the same problem with squatters that they were having at the Widow Maker. "Hey, you never did tell me what you knew about the Cusslers. I tried to look them up this morning, but it doesn't appear that they have left much of a paper trail."

"I don't know much, just what Gwen told me in passing."

"So she knew there were people living out there in the boondocks?"

Sabrina passed him a guilty look.

He wasn't sure if he should be annoyed that his cousin hadn't taken care of the problem before they arrived, or if he should be concerned. Gwen must have known the danger. Maybe she had avoided them out of fear.

He just loved walking into a hornet's nest.

"Do you know how many folks we should be worried about out there?"

"From what I know, which isn't too much, it sounds like there were just some brothers. I'm assuming that the man we found is one of them."

"Were any of the brothers married?" he asked.

"I don't know. They were all pretty reclusive, but with that came an ability to live off the land. Whoever is left out there, they are certainly more than capable of surviving."

He nodded. He wasn't worried about their ability to survive—in fact, he was about as far away from that concern as humanly possible. They were just looking for more potential threats. Hopefully he wouldn't tangle with the remaining brothers, their wives, kids, grandkids, dogs and who knew who or what else. He had been in that situation before. Family dynamics always had a way of complicating any situation.

When they found the rest of the clan—rather, if they found them—he could speak to them and discover what happened. Maybe he was making something out of nothing. Maybe the Cusslers had gotten in a fight, and the man he'd found had been on the losing end. Hopefully, this had nothing to do with the Gray Wolves, or Trevor's family's long-term safety.

"I'm not sure if you're aware," Sabrina started, sounding nervous, "but Gwen's husband, Wyatt, is the local sheriff's deputy here."

"Sabrina, can I ask you something?" As he asked, he second-guessed himself.

"Hmm?" she said, looking over at him and away from the road.

"I appreciate you not wanting to make waves with this guy's death…but why—"

Her face pinched as she interrupted him. "Let's just say that I don't want to draw any unnecessary attention."

"Why? Are you on the run from the law or something?"

She laughed, but the sound was tight. "Hardly. I just don't like drama. I've had enough of that over the last couple of years." She tapped her fingers on the steering wheel nervously. "And as much as I think murderers should be held accountable, this guy didn't seem like the type that would want someone digging too deeply into his life."

To a certain degree, he agreed with her. However, everything just felt off about her answer. She was hiding something.

"If you don't mind me asking, what kind of drama have you been going through?"

She nibbled at her lip, like she was deciding whether to tell him the truth. It all came down to this—if she opened up to him he would finally be able to trust her. If she didn't, well…

"Let's just say I found myself in a relationship with the worst possible man."

Oh.

She was wounded. Now she was beginning to make a little more sense to him. He could understand some of the fear and pain she was feeling.

"I get it." It was the only thing he could think to say. What he really wanted to do was to pull her into his arms and make her feel better. Together, they could heal from the traumas of their past.

Sabrina chuckled. "What about you—any skeletons in your closet?"

He visibly twitched but tried to cover it up by casually scratching at his neck. He wasn't sure he was ready to tell her about his own failed relationships. "I…I used to be married."

Instead of coming at him with questions, as he assumed she would, she sat in silence for a long time letting the road roll by.

"I hope you know you can trust me," she said, finally breaking the silence between them.

This time he didn't even try to cover up his twitch. There was no way she could possibly read his mind, and yet here they were. "The rifle at the head of my bed…"

She tensed, her hands wrapping tight around the steering wheel until her knuckles were white. "Yeah, I was going to ask you about that."

At least she wasn't denying or trying to hide the fact that she had gotten into his gun case. He could respect her honesty.

"I spent quite a few years in the army before we started in the investments game. I guess some old habits die hard."

He was grateful as a ranch came into view in the distance. There was a long row of stables, a main house and a bright red barn. The place looked like something out of *Town & Country* magazine. "Is that Dunrovin?"

Sabrina nodded. "You should see this place at Christmas. Gwen showed me some pictures of last year's Yule Night Festival. There were Christmas lights everywhere, the whole shebang."

He had no idea what the Yule Night thing was, but he was glad they were no longer talking about their pasts.

As they drove up and parked in the gravel lot of the ranch, a group of mutts ran out to greet them. Well, mostly mutts. Among them was a small Chihuahua barking maniacally at their approach. In fact, the little dog seemed to be the leader of the pack, egging on the rest of them in their cacophony.

"Looks like we got the royal greeting," he said with a chuckle.

An older woman walked out from the ranch's office, waving at them as they approached. Behind her was a woman with long, wild blond hair whom he recognized as his cousin Gwen. He hadn't seen her since they were children, but even the way she moved, with an air of confidence and grace, hadn't really changed.

The older woman called the dogs off and herded them into the office, closing the door behind the pack and then turning back to Trevor and Sabrina. "Welcome to Dunrovin. It's a pleasure to finally get the chance to meet you, Trevor. I've heard so much about you from Gwen," she said, extending her hand as he made his way up the steps.

"The pleasure is all mine..." He shook her hand as he waited for her to supply him with her name. Hopefully all she had heard about him had been positive.

When he and Gwen had last met, when they were both about eight years old. He had pulled her pigtails, which had quickly devolved into a wrestling match that ended with them both muddy messes. He could still distinctly remember the hay sticking out of Gwen's French braids and the stupid, victorious smile on her face.

"Eloise. Eloise Fitzgerald," the silver-haired woman said, giving his hand a strong shake.

"Hey guys," Gwen said with a nod. "I already have the horses waiting for you in the trailer. Are you sure you don't want me to go along with you on your ride? I know some great Forest Service trails. There's one up Elk Meadows you would love."

Eloise jabbed a sharp-looking elbow into Gwen's ribs and looked back and forth between him and Sabrina, like she was seeing something between them that wasn't there.

"Oh," he said with a chuckle. "We…no…"

"It's not that kind of ride," Sabrina said, finishing his sentence for him. "We are just going to go out and check some fences, then maybe head up the mountain for a couple of hours."

Gwen frowned. "The fences were in good order when I left."

Eloise looked over at her like she was clearly not getting the hint. "Don't worry about it, Gwen. You and I have plenty of things to do in the office today. In fact, I was hoping you could call next week's guests and confirm their reservations. Then we need to finalize the menus and talk to the kitchen staff."

Thank goodness for busy work.

"I'll be waiting for you in the office," Eloise said, motioning inside. "Shortly."

Gwen nodded as Eloise gave them a quick, knowing wave and made her way into the office. She was met with a barrage of barking.

"I hope you don't mind taking the old ranch pickup," Gwen said, walking them out toward the barn where a white pickup and horse trailer were waiting. As they grew nearer, there was the thump of hooves coming from the trailer. "I already put their saddles on, but you're going to need to cinch them tighter when you get there." She looked him up and down as though she doubted his abilities. "Are you sure you can handle this? If you need, you can give me a call and I can help you out."

He waved her off. He hadn't been riding in a long time, but he was sure that after a couple of minutes he'd be more than comfortable back in the saddle. "Nah, but thanks. If I need something, I'll just give you a ring."

"Just so you know, about half the back side of the Widow Maker is without cell reception—or it's sporadic at best. Make sure you're careful out there," Gwen said, giving Sabrina a look of concern. "If Trevor is anything like he was when we were kids, he's going to go all out and get himself into trouble. He tends to act first and ask questions later."

He laughed, the sound coming from deep in his core. "I'm not a kid anymore. You don't need to worry about me."

"I'm not worried about you," Gwen said, stepping closer to Sabrina. "I have this girl's life and the welfare of our horses to be concerned about."

Though she was just teasing, he couldn't help being rankled by her ribbing. "Look, if you don't want us to take the horses, it's okay. We can find some other way to do the work. Chad and I have been talking about getting four-wheelers. I was just putting it off until we knew exactly what—"

"Stop. It's okay," Gwen said, interrupting him. "I just want you to remember that we are in Montana, not New York. Everything isn't just a phone call away. I don't want you to go messing around up there and find yourselves in trouble. Believe it or not I love you, cousin."

"I love you, too, even if you are still a pain in my ass." He laughed as he wrapped his arm around her and gave her a quick side hug. "Hey, about the Cusslers... Sabrina said you knew a bit about them."

Gwen nodded, smoothing her shirt where it had wrinkled under his touch. As she moved, he spotted the band on her finger. "They would come to mind with the mention of a pain in the ass, wouldn't they?" Gwen sighed. "What did they do now? I want you to know, I tried to talk to them when I found out you were going to take over the ranch. They were less than welcoming."

Apparently, they had all been alive, which was more than he was currently working with. Yet he couldn't let Gwen know anything that would implicate her should something leak to the authorities.

"I believe it," he said, stabbing the toe of his boot into the gravel of the parking lot. "How many are living out there?"

She shrugged. "All I know for sure is that there were four brothers and a couple of women. But there could be more or less. They were a bit like rats, scurrying around and hiding whenever we went out there to try to talk to them."

Which meant that they may well have been around when he and Sabrina had gone out to evict them. He could understand exactly why they had been living out there for so long. It was hard to catch their kind.

He glanced over toward Sabrina, who gave him an acknowledging nod. Her face was pinched, like she was working hard to keep a secret, and somehow that simple look made something shift inside him... something like trust clicking into place. No, it was something else, something deeper, a feeling much too close to desire.

Like before, he wanted to tell her to relax and that everything would be all right, but if he'd learned anything in the last few months, it was that no one close to him ever walked away unharmed.

He couldn't allow himself to fall for her. And if he couldn't stop himself, he most certainly couldn't allow her to get any closer to him than she already was. If he could, he would fire her and send her far from this place...but Chad would have his hide.

"Do you know about how old they all were?" Sabrina asked.

Gwen shook her head. "The oldest brother was probably around forty. And the women... I don't know if they were wives or sisters, but they could have been anywhere between their twenties and forties. From the state of them, it was hard to tell."

"What do you mean?" Trevor asked.

Gwen twitched. "They hadn't bathed in a long time. Their hair was in mats. They looked absolutely wild. We wanted to help them, but what could we do? We were barely making it as it was. And like I said, the Cusslers were well beyond wanting or taking help."

"I get it, Gwen. After seeing their place…" Trevor stopped as he tried to prevent the memory of the dead man's sallow face from creeping into his mind. "Do you know if they get along?"

Gwen nibbled at her bottom lip. "From what I know and what my husband has said, it seemed as though they do. But there are whispers that there are other groups out there—families like the Cusslers who take to the hills."

"Do you know where they're living?"

She shrugged. "Nomads for the most part. The Cusslers just managed to find a spot to squat where they didn't face too much trouble."

"So they don't move around at all?" Sabrina asked.

"I think they may have a hunting cabin farther up the ridge. I assume they went up there whenever they were needing a fresh supply of game."

Trevor checked his excitement. Just because they found a possible location for the rest of the Cusslers didn't mean they were any closer to finding out who had killed the man.

"Now, I don't know if there is any validity to it, but I heard rumblings from Wyatt that the Cusslers were fighting another family out there. From the sounds of it, it was a real Hatfields-and-McCoys kind of thing—doesn't sound like there were ever any kind of winners." Gwen glanced toward the mountains that loomed over them. "It was just another reason for us to keep our distance, the last thing we wanted to do was get wrapped up in a never-ending war."

He held back a chuckle. His entire life was just one unending war. Whether it was here or on the banks of the Yangtze River, he'd always be fighting some kind of battle, but at least these kinds weren't the ones inside him.

He relaxed slightly.

If Gwen was right, they had nothing to worry about. The man was a victim of nothing more than a hillbilly civil war. But if she was wrong…if the Gray Wolves had planted a false rumor…

No, they wouldn't. It was too far-fetched. The Gray Wolves were smart, but like him, they wouldn't just walk into this community and start stirring up trouble. They would want to fly under the radar.

But he couldn't make another catastrophic mistake when it came to his family's safety—he couldn't live with himself if he lost someone else because of his failure to understand his enemy.

Eloise poked her head out of the office door. "Gwen, you coming?"

She tossed him the keys and he scooped them out of the air. "Thanks, Gwen."

She dipped her head. "Not a problem. Just be careful out there. I don't have a good feeling about this." She turned to walk away, but looked back at them. "You aren't planning to go out there to see the Cusslers today, are you?"

Sabrina slipped her hand into his, their skin brushing as she took the keys from him.

"Nah," he said, but even to his ears it came out sounding tinny and fake as he looked down to the place where Sabrina had touched him. "Fences today. Just wanted to know what to expect."

Gwen gave him a wide smile, like she actually believed his lie.

Denial just might have been his most powerful ally—especially when it came to his own feelings.

Chapter Six

Sabrina gripped the steering wheel hard, carefully maneuvering the truck and horse trailer down the bumpy road leading straight to the Cusslers' shanty. Every time the truck hit a bump and the mud splattered against the windshield, she cursed last night's rain, and she couldn't help but to look over at Trevor to see if he was silently judging her.

Truth be told, she hadn't driven a truck carrying such a heavy load before, but she would never be second to a man. She could do anything he could. She was tough. And what she didn't know, she would learn.

"Are you sure you don't want me to drive?" Trevor asked, holding on to the dashboard like it was his lifeline.

She gritted her teeth. "I've got this." As she spoke, the front right tire connected with a giant rock in the road, jarring them so hard it made her jump in the seat.

"Dude," Trevor said, looking back at the horse trailer they were pulling. "If you're not careful, you're going to end up rolling us."

Though she was only going ten miles an hour, she slowed the truck down even more. "Look, Trevor, if you think you can drive better than I can on this crap, be my guest. But it's not as easy as it looks." She motioned toward the muddy, pitted road in front of them. "Have you ever even driven a truck and trailer before?"

He opened his mouth to speak, but paused for a long moment as he stared at her. "I've done more of this kind of driving than I care to admit."

This was her chance—finally she could learn more about this man in a way that wouldn't seem suspicious.

"All that driving have anything to do with that gun I found in your bedroom?" she asked, raising an eyebrow.

He snickered. "You're awful curious, aren't you?"

Or maybe it wasn't her opening, after all.

"I just like to know who I'm working for…and whether I need to be concerned for my safety or not."

He slowly blinked, like he was trying his hardest to control every single muscle in his body. "The only people who should be scared of me are my enemies. You've already shown me that we are fighting on the same side. In all honesty, it's been a long time since I've been around somebody—other than my family—who hasn't wanted to use me to achieve their own gains. It's a bit of a relief."

A wave of guilt washed over her. Sometimes she hated the duality of her job. Here she was making strides professionally, and yet she found herself personally compromised. It would've been so much easier if she didn't like the man she been sent here to investigate.

Then again, perhaps his little speech was nothing more than a subtle manipulation, a tactic to lull her into becoming complacent. Well, if he thought she would be that easy to manipulate, he was wrong.

Or maybe she was just looking for a reason to stop herself from falling for Trevor. It was unprofessional in every way, to even think about having feelings for the handsome man sitting beside her in the truck. Yet a heart wanted what a heart wanted; if her heart was easily controlled by her mind, she would never have found herself in the backwoods of Montana.

This time had to be different. She couldn't let herself be sucked in by a man's charms; she had to remain distant. Untouchable.

"With time, Trevor, you'll find that I'm a woman who is different from the rest. I'm not the type to pander to a guy."

Trevor took his hands off the dashboard and leaned back in his seat, like he was trying to avoid the ricochet of her words within the truck's cabin.

"You don't think I was already aware of that?" Trevor asked.

"Well, I just don't want you thinking that I was…" She paused as she searched for the right word. "I guess I don't want you to assume that I'm weak. You know, after what happened the first time we came down here to the Cusslers' place. I don't know what came over me. This time when we see this guy, I'll be ready."

Trevor looked at her for a long moment, almost as if he was trying to decide how to proceed. "Sabrina, it's okay to have a weakness."

There was a softness in his voice that made her wonder if there wasn't another layer of meaning to his words.

"Weakness is unacceptable. Weakness means we have to depend on those around us. Doing something like that means you open yourself up for disappointment, for hurt. Strength is the only way to survive."

"Do you mean in dating, or in life?" Trevor asked, as his hand slid slowly to the center of the bench seat.

"Both," she said, jerking the wheel as she dramatically tried to avoid another pothole, secretly wishing he'd be forced to hold on again so his hand wouldn't be so accessible. A girl only had so much restraint.

"Don't take offense, but…" Trevor sighed. "Well, you sound like a woman who's been hurt…a lot."

She answered with a dark chuckle. "If you had

grown up in a family like mine, you'd see the world from my perspective, too."

"You mean because your family was military?" Trevor asked.

She was surprised he remembered anything about her. She'd have to be careful about what exactly she said to him. "The moving around and constant change was fine. Sure, it takes a special breed to be able to live that kind of lifestyle, but that wasn't what our problems really stemmed from. My dad was the kind who always wanted to be in control, and sometimes that meant acting in a way that is completely unacceptable by today's standards."

"Is that why you took the truck keys from me— you wanted to remain in control?"

"I took the truck keys because I saw you driving the other day. I wanted no part of that." She laughed.

The smile returned to Trevor's face and his hand moved a bit closer. "One time is not indicative of anything." He reached over and took her hand, like he finally was giving up on her making the first move.

His hand felt cool against hers, and she wasn't sure if it was because he was cold or if she was just blazing hot because of her nerves. She thought about disentangling their fingers, but as he started to caress her skin she couldn't find the willpower.

It felt so good to be touched. It was strange, but besides their hug the other day, it had been a long time since anyone really touched her. More, she was being touched by Trevor…the only man she had ever been instantly attracted to.

With most men, her attraction to them only occurred after months of them being securely planted in the friend zone. She hadn't really taken Mike's advances seriously for at least six months; that was until Mike had finally kissed her after a lunch meeting, and something inside her changed.

This thing with Trevor, it was…disconcerting, uncomfortable and strange. And yet so right. When she looked at him, she wanted to move closer. To touch more of him. To feel his arms around her. It was like he was the sun on her face after months of winter gray. As much as she loved the sensation, that spark, she hated it.

Many of her friends had told her stories about the elusive spark, and how they knew the instant they met someone that they loved them. All their talk had made her wonder if there wasn't something wrong with her—aside from her atrocious taste in her past boyfriends. She had tried to make herself feel better by telling herself that her friends were crazy, that nothing like that ever existed except in movies. Those sparks were just weakness…their body's way of opening itself up and revealing its most vulnerable part—the heart.

Right now, she wasn't sure if she was right or wrong, but she wasn't ready to give her heart to anyone…not after all she had put it through in the last few years.

"I'm a good driver, regardless of what you think." She forced herself to let go of his hand.

A silence widened the gap between them.

"Uh-huh," he said, sounding dejected as he put his hand in his lap.

Maybe it had been wrong to pull back from him. If she had stayed put it might have made it easier to learn everything she needed to know about his family, their work, their role in the murders and their gun trade. And for a while, she could have just lied to herself and told herself that this really was her life. She could play the housekeeper who was falling head over heels for the man beside her.

She groaned. Why did he have to make her feel this way? It was so much easier to live within the framework built by the FBI—where he was nothing but her assignment and she was safely detached.

If feelings didn't have a way of muddling everything in her life maybe they wouldn't be so bad, but as it was, feelings sucked.

As the little shanty came into view, with its rusty, corrugated steel roof filled with holes, she relaxed. She'd never been so happy to get to a dead body in her life. At least she'd have something to think about besides her feelings.

That was, if she could just control her reaction when she saw the man again. She couldn't be weak in front of Trevor. She had to prove to him that, like he said, a single event wasn't truly indicative of any-thing—it was an anomaly.

She pulled the truck and trailer down the drive leading to the pathetic shack and turned to Trevor. "I'll get the horses together and buttoned up if you want to go take a look around."

He gave her a look of disbelief, like he questioned who she thought she was giving orders to him. She'd have to reel that in a bit. No matter what she person-ally felt, she had to remember that she was supposed to be doing a job…a job that didn't include leading the charge in getting to the bottom of a hillbilly's murder mystery. She had bigger fish to fry.

"If you don't mind, I'll give you a hand," Trevor said. "With things out here so up in the air, I don't want to leave you alone. We don't know where those other Cussler boys are, or the women. For all we know, we're walking out into some kind of moun-tain men's civil war."

He wasn't wrong, but she couldn't seem to think straight thanks to his presence.

"You think his body's still inside?" she asked.

Trevor shrugged. "I'd be lying if I said I hoped his body was still in there. It would make things a lot easier if his remains are buried somewhere out in the woods."

Once again, they were skating down the slippery

slope between right and wrong, but she couldn't disagree with him.

The horses nickered as she and Trevor stepped out of the truck and into the mud. Theirs were the only fresh tracks.

"It's okay, guys, we're gonna get you out," Trevor cooed to the horses as they stomped inside the trailer.

He walked around behind the trailer and opened the door. Carefully, they backed the horses out and walked them around and tied them up. He helped her put on the horse's bridle and cinch her saddle tight. He may not have gone on a horseback ride in a long time, but he seemed right at home taking care of the animals.

"Here, let me give you a leg up," he said, holding out his hands.

She didn't want to take his help. Not after she'd made such a show of taking over the driving. But the last time she'd ridden on a horse the owner had kindly given her a set of steps in order to get up.

She put her left foot in the stirrup and he helped her with her right. For a moment, his hand rested on her thigh as he untied the horse and handed her the reins, unclipping the lead rope.

"You got him. You gonna be okay?" he asked.

She nodded. She'd forgotten the thrill that came with sitting astride a horse. It didn't escape her that she was sitting on an animal who weighed a ton more than she did, but was just as stubborn. Hopefully today would go well and she wouldn't make an idiot of herself. All she had to do was pretend she knew what she was doing and soon enough she would.

At least she hoped.

"What's her name?" she asked as the horse took an unwelcome step away from the trailer. She checked the reins, trying to pull her to a stop.

"First off, he's a gelding, and I think he goes by Zane."

She wasn't off to a great start.

She ran her hands down his whiskey-colored coat. "You and I are going to get along great, aren't we, Zane?" She tried to sound more confident than she felt.

The horse took another step, and she tried to relax into the saddle. It was going to be okay; she just had to play it cool.

Trevor rode up alongside her. "And this is Donnie. They're both supposed to be great horses, so I think you're gonna do fine." He reached back and slipped something into the saddlebag.

Apparently, he could see exactly how uncomfortable she was. She readjusted herself in the saddle and tried to recall what she had been told about sitting up straight. She couldn't remember exactly how she was supposed to move with the horse. No doubt she looked like a sixth-grade girl at her first dance—gangly and out of rhythm.

And just like a sixth-grade girl, she wondered

when she would finally get over her awkwardness. She was tired of always feeling like she didn't quite fit into any situation. Just once, she would've liked to let herself go and fully give herself to the world around her.

Thankfully, Trevor and Donnie took the lead and Zane moved in step behind them. They rode over to the shanty, where Trevor stepped down from his horse and handed her his reins. "You guys stay here and I'll go check on our friend. I'll be right back."

She looped the reins in her hand and stared at the cabin's blacked-out window. For a second, she considered getting down and going in with Trevor, but she stayed seated. Maybe it was weak of her to not want to see the dead man, but it saved her from making a fool of herself. It was probably the same reason Trevor had left her behind.

She couldn't deny the fact that he was thoughtful and kind, but she forced the thoughts away. No, he was a fugitive from the law. Her enemy.

She pulled out her phone—no signal. She hated the feeling of being cut off from the world around her. There probably wouldn't be a cell signal again until they were back at the ranch. She reminded herself that they'd be back tonight. Besides, Mike had made it clear that he wasn't keen on the idea of her checking in too often. If she was out of contact, at least she would be off Mike's radar.

And yet the whole situation made the hair on the

back of her neck stand on end. She was completely on her own. If Trevor caught even a whiff of what she was up to, he could kill her and dump her body without anyone ever being the wiser.

She took a calming breath. No, she hadn't made him suspect anything. This would go fine. It would be suspicious if she tried to leave now. She just had to blend in and play along, gleaning information as they went.

There was the rattle of dishes from inside the cabin. "Everything okay in there?" she called.

"Yeah, everything's fine," Trevor answered. "The body's gone. Aside from him being missing, everything else seems untouched." Trevor walked out of the cabin and got back up into the saddle. He was frowning, and there was a distinct look of concern on his face.

"I bet it was one of the brothers. They probably saw us here the other day and as soon as we left they came in and got the body."

She thought back to the puddle of blood she'd destroyed behind the shanty. More than likely, the blood had belonged to one of the other Cusslers, and it wasn't until he'd been treated for his wound that the family could come and recover the body. And yet she couldn't tell Trevor what she really thought.

Trevor rode toward the trail that led up the mountain. "The only way we can be sure to know what is going on here is to find them. We need to talk to them and make sure they know they aren't welcome back. I can't have my family involved with whatever's going on out here. We don't do chaos."

She nearly chuckled. Her life was often nothing but chaos and one crazy event after another—just another reason they didn't fit. Not to mention she would be constantly keeping secrets from him. A relationship and life built on bedlam and secrets wasn't viable—she had learned that lesson all too well. And in her line of work, all she had was secrets. She could only imagine what would happen if she truly had to keep everything about her work away from the man she loved.

Wait, did she love him? No. It was impossible.

She had to pay attention to the work at hand and remember that she was going to bring chaos to his life no matter what he wanted.

"What else have you found out about their family?" she asked as they started ascending the trail.

"My sister, Zoey, she's a super nerd. Anything on the computer, she can do it," he said, his tone filled with unmistakable love and pride for her. "She's been looking into a few things for me, and so far, we haven't found anything of use. Though I can't say I was surprised."

"She found nothing. That's odd."

"There was just one headline, must have been from forty years ago—a man who might have been the dead guy's father was convicted on a murder charge. Apparently, he suffered from what the paper called insanity, but from what I can make of it, it sounded like he had undiagnosed schizophrenia. He spent ten years in an institution, then disappeared from the records."

She cringed as she thought of the antiquated institutions where those with mental health issues had been stuffed away. They were the thing of nightmares—corporal punishment, physical labor, isolation, lobotomies and even sometimes practicing eugenics. She could barely imagine the horror and the terror those who were forced to live in such a place must have experienced.

"As in he died? Or do you think he escaped?"

Trevor shrugged. "I would guess he died, but who knows."

Even if the man was alive, by now he'd have to be in at least his late sixties, and the last thing he would do is kill his own son. But then again, humans—and the atrocities they committed—constantly surprised her. Filicide wasn't that uncommon, even if she wasn't accustomed to seeing it. She'd heard about it in many other investigations—and it was increasingly common in cases where large amounts of money or corporations were involved…or in cases of mental illness.

On the other hand, she'd read study after study that had found that only a small proportion of schizophrenics were dangerous to others…and yet this man had already proven that he was in the small percentage that was willing to kill.

She nibbled at her lip. If she remembered correctly, children of a person with schizophrenia were 13 percent more likely to develop symptoms of the disease.

"Do you think he was killed by family, or do you really think it was someone else? One of the other squatter families?"

The leather of his saddle creaked as he looked back at her. "I hope it's one of those things. If not, we're going to have a significantly bigger problem on our hands."

"What are you going to do if these guys come back to the shack?" she asked.

"We will make sure they know they aren't welcome...we can't have people being murdered left and right on our land and we can't be compromised—" He stopped and glanced back at her to see if she was listening. "We can't have anyone or anything living at the ranch that is going to be a liability."

She tried to keep from cringing. "Gwen and her mother lived here for a long time. They managed to coexist peacefully with the Cusslers. Don't you think it's strange that all of a sudden people are turning up dead out here?"

"Gwen didn't tell you everything, did she?" He laughed. "Gwen's crew called the cops out here more times than I can count to evict the family. When that didn't work, they came out and bulldozed their little shanty—more than once. These suckers are like gophers. They just keep popping their heads up."

In a way, she couldn't help but feel sorry for the people who had been living out here on the land illegally; no doubt, if they had other options, they wouldn't have found themselves in the situation they were in. But perhaps she was giving the Cusslers too much credit. They were knowingly breaking the law, indifferent about the rights of others, disrespectful and possible killers.

She shook her head as she thought of the moral pluralism they were facing. Why could nothing be cut-and-dried? What she would give to go back in time, to live in her early twenties when she was smart and resourceful enough to be independent, but still naive enough to believe that everything in the world was simply black or white, good or evil. She longed for the days when she just made a decision and didn't second-guess herself or think of at least nineteen other ways to answer the questions posed to her.

"I'm sure Gwen doesn't feel good about what she was forced to do," she said, thinking of the moment she covered up the blood, and when she had come inside the shanty to see Trevor wiping off the gun.

"Like Gwen said, they were well beyond help." Trevor slowed down so they could ride side by side.

The terrain had flattened out and they were surrounded by a thick pine forest, a forest where anything or anyone could have been hiding completely undetected. Chills rippled down her spine as she thought of the danger that may well have been surrounding them. Trevor reached down and ran his fingers over his gun's grip as he also must have realized the farther they rode, the farther they were from help.

"Had you ever been to the house before, you know, before we saw *him*?" she asked.

Trevor shook his head. "No, but I'd heard about the place and I had been tasked with cleaning it up—just like you."

Was that what he had been doing with the murder weapon—cleaning up the place?

She wanted to ask him why he had wiped off the gun, but if she revealed what she had seen, it may well place her in danger. Trevor would never hurt her, but she didn't know if she could say the same thing about the rest of his family. If it was known she could act as a witness and testify against him—if push came to shove—they may decide to take her out. As it was, he had already hinted that they saw her as some kind of liability.

She was the only one outside the family, and outside the Cusslers, who knew about the murder.

She had known she was in danger before, but as she worked through her thoughts, the fear within her swelled.

"Is that why you picked up the gun and wiped it

off?" If she was going to be in danger, she might as well at least find out the truth.

Trevor pulled his horse to a stop and she followed suit. He stared at her for a long moment, like he was thinking about exactly what he wanted to say. He had to realize there was no use in lying; obviously she had seen what he had done, and he was likely weighing the consequences and ramifications of her revelation.

"I don't know why I did that. I just—"

"Wanted to cover your brother's tracks?" she said, finishing his sentence.

"Look, I don't know where you got that idea, but Chad isn't the kind of guy who would just come out and murder somebody. We aren't that kind of people…we're just looking for a quiet place to retire and get out of the public eye." Trevor raised his hands, like he was submitting to her.

She wanted to believe him, but he and his family were likely nothing but a deadly force.

"But you weren't sure, or else you wouldn't wipe down the gun. There was no harm in just leaving it there if you knew he wasn't responsible."

He looked down at his hands as he rested them on the saddle horn.

"From the little time I've been here, it's obvious to me you guys aren't all you say you are—you're not just some investment bankers or hedge fund family or whatever." Her entire body tensed as she thought about how much danger she was putting herself in.

"Who is it that you think we are?" Trevor asked, catching her gaze. He looked torn.

"I don't know, but I want you to tell me." She was forcing him to completely trust her or else get rid of her.

She was playing the odds that he had strong feelings for her, feelings that he would give in to. It was just too bad that if he did open up to her, he'd end up getting screwed.

Chapter Seven

The last person who started asking questions about his family had ended up dead. It had been three weeks before the body washed ashore on the coast of North Carolina. They handled security breaches in such a way that he was surprised anyone had ever found the body at all.

He couldn't let anything happen to Sabrina. She wasn't like the man before, who had been investigating the family for the French government. She was innocent and unfortunately too observant and smart for her own good—and for his as well.

"My family and I are from New York. Last year, our tech company VidCon went public and we sold our shares to an investor. We all had been working together for so long it just didn't make sense for us to go our separate ways, and we all loved the Widow Maker. We came here a lot as children and had so many good memories. Here, we could be together as a family, each building our own houses on the property."

He looked over at her to see if she was buying his story. From the sour look on her face, she wasn't.

"I know that's who you say you are, but most tech junkies I've met don't have sniper rifles in their bedroom. Not to mention a closet full of military gear." She looked at him like he was growing two heads. "I'm not an idiot, Trevor."

"Yes, I was in the military. Where do you think I learned how to run logistics for a company?" He had to make her believe the story he was selling, otherwise she'd be toast.

She nudged her horse forward, making him wonder if she just couldn't stand being so close to him any longer. He wanted to reach out and pull her back to him, to tell her to stop thinking what she was thinking, that she was wandering down a dangerous path—but he couldn't.

"I know you're not telling me something, Trevor. You don't have to keep lying to me. I want to help." As she spoke, he couldn't help but notice that she wasn't looking at him.

They rode in silence as they moved off the property and onto public lands, Sabrina leading the way, for at least three miles. He didn't know exactly where they were going, but it didn't matter; he needed all the time he could get in order to make a decision about what to do with her.

If he were smart, he would take care of the problem that she was becoming with a single shot. He'd hate himself for it, but he needed to protect his family. They had to come first—they always came first. The dedication and loyalty they had for one another was the reason they had survived in the business as long as they had. He couldn't let a woman come between them.

And yet there was something about her that he was inexplicably drawn to. Sabrina was the last thing he had expected when he'd learned that she was the family's housekeeper. She didn't seem to fit the bill of someone who would want to make her living by cleaning up after people. She seemed like the kind of woman who would find that monotonous. If anything, she seemed like a fit for a job like a district attorney or something…a job that would require she be able to speak her piece and then back it up with statistics and charts.

He could imagine her up in front of a judge and jury, arguing for the greater good. She'd definitely put him on the spot about that gun…and in doing so, she seemed to understand that she was going to draw scrutiny. And yet she still had the strength to face him head-on. That ability both captivated and terrified him.

"Sabrina," he said, finally breaking the silence between them as he rode up alongside her, "don't be upset with me. I'm sorry about what happened with the gun. I made a mistake. Just know it was made with the best intentions."

She sighed, letting the clatter of their horses' footfalls against the rocky scree path fill the air. "I appreciate your apology, but I don't like feeling like I'm being lied to. And if you're like me…or if you're feeling what I'm feeling…" She reached over and took his hand, the simple action surprising him. "You have to understand that all I really want is for you to open up to me."

He wanted to do that, to tell her everything about who he was, what he'd seen and where he'd been. He wanted someone to tell his fears to and his dreams, but that wasn't his life. It wasn't something he could offer another person. His life was complicated, so much so that regardless of what his heart wanted, he couldn't risk bringing another person in.

And yet he couldn't deny that he was feeling something for her—something he hadn't felt for a woman in a long time.

Not for the first time since her death, Trevor wished he could go to Trish to ask her advice. She would've known exactly what to do and the kinds of questions to ask. He missed her so much. His brothers and Zoey were great, but none of them had a relationship like he'd had with Trish. With her, he'd always been able to talk about anything—even feelings. He didn't delve into them often, and now that Trish was gone, he wasn't sure he was really up to talking about feelings ever again. They were just so damned complicated, especially when it came to the other sex.

"Sabrina, have you had a lot of serious relationships? I know you said you'd had a rough time with the last guy you dated, but have you dated anyone else for a long time?" *Ugh*. That had not come out at all like he'd wanted it to. It sounded so stupid.

She glanced over at him with a cheeky grin on her face. "I do know what a serious relationship is, Trevor." She laughed. "And yes, I've had a couple serious relationships. Why?"

"When you were in these relationships, did you always tell them everything?"

The grin on her face twitched. "What are you getting at, Trevor?" Her voice lost its playful edge.

He'd struck a nerve. She must have been hiding something about her love life. Maybe that's why she had come to the middle of nowhere to disappear. He'd dated enough in his lifetime that he could certainly understand the desire. There was nothing worse than heartbreak.

At least he wasn't the only one with a secret.

"I'm not saying that I think you're a liar or anything," Trevor said. "I'm just asking if there are things you choose not to tell—" *the person you love*.

He didn't dare finish his sentence. He was already close to implying that their relationship was something more. She didn't love him; she barely knew him. And yet…ever since they'd met he hadn't wanted to be without her. It was like her presence both comforted him and made him question everything. It reminded him of the first time he'd fallen in love, but then he'd been merely a teenager—he couldn't go back to being the boy he once was. He'd had too much happen in his life, too many heartbreaks and failed relationships. He couldn't allow himself to repeat his mistakes.

Her grin reappeared. "I admit nothing."

"Admit it or not, we both know that no relationship is completely without secrets. Sometimes in order to keep a friendship or relationship, or to make another person feel better, we omit things. It's human nature."

"Human nature or not, what you did at the shanty was more than just omitting a detail." She paused. "But here's the deal, I don't want you to lie—ever. I don't want you to omit anything. I want to be able to trust you."

Here he'd been worrying about trusting her, and apparently she'd been worried about trusting him as well. That made him chuckle. Maybe they were more alike than he thought.

As they moved higher up the mountain, snow dusted the scree. Even in August and September, snow was common in the high country, and it wasn't unheard of to get fresh snow in the higher elevations every month of the year.

Though he had brought a few essentials, in case of emergency, he didn't have enough supplies to last more than a day or two at most. When it got dark, and colder, the snow was likely to become a problem.

He didn't want to put Sabrina at risk. If something went awry, or if he got hurt, he didn't want to burden her with all that it would take for them to survive.

He thought back to his days in Afghanistan. At that time, he'd just gotten into the private security game with his family. They'd been at it for some time, but he'd finally reached an age at which his father agreed to bring him along. Being out there, in the countryside of a foreign nation where he didn't speak the language or know the customs, had been intimidating. It hadn't taken him long to learn that what they did tended to get people killed.

He winced, remembering the al-Qaeda hit man who got gunned down right in front of him for failing to light his commander's cigarette. Later his brothers had explained to him the commander had done it as a show of force, as a reminder that they were to do as he wished and play by his rules. The man had died because they were there.

He'd had to stay at that camp, pretending to be a bodyguard for the al-Qaeda commander, for two months. Luckily, he had gotten out of there alive. It had been one hell of a welcome into STEALTH.

After he left, they had traced the terrorist group coordinates thanks to the implanted GPS trackers in the weapons they had supplied. Some of the guns had spread as far north as Mirzaki and as far south as Bahram Chah. With the information they had accumulated, they gave the coordinates of the largest and most active terrorist cells to the DO, or directorate of operations. The next day, eight of the ten cells had been wiped off the map.

It wasn't the easiest or the cleanest way to track the movements of their enemies, but it had been highly effective. They were proof that boots on the ground were truly their government's most effective weapon. He was sure that they had saved thousands of lives.

What he'd done then was a thousand times more challenging than what he had to do now. And yet finding himself alone with Sabrina seemed to create an entirely new level of difficulty. Maybe it would be easier if they just dispelled the sexual tension that reverberated between them. If they just kissed, things would get easier, and hell…maybe he could go back to focusing on the task at hand. He kept finding himself thinking about them, about her, trust and feelings and not thinking about where they were or what they needed to be looking for. At this rate, unless the hunting camp had been built right in the middle of the game trail, he doubted he would notice it.

"Do you want to turn back?" he said, his breath making a cloud in the cold.

Her cheeks were red, like they had been nibbled

at by the chill of the later afternoon. "No, I'm fine." Her words were slow.

"Let's take a little break." When they came up to a flat clearing, he got off his horse and held out his hand to Sabrina. Her fingers felt like ice.

He had to build a fire before hypothermia got the better of her. It had to be in the twenties, with snow starting to accumulate around them. While the snow would prove helpful in tracking, he had to get his head on straight before he was ready to continue.

Heck, maybe he was right in thinking about turning back. She was cold; he wasn't at the top of his game.

She hugged her arms around herself and did a little two-step move as she tried to get warm.

Yes, fire first.

He tied the horses up to a couple of pines and set about collecting anything dry that would burn. He made his way back to her with a collection of pine needles, pitch wood and branches. She had built a little teepee-shaped stack on the ground with her own collection of fire starters. A tendril of smoke was already puffing from the top of the stack, and there was a split log sitting beside it.

She looked up at him as the fire got going. "Oh, hey, thanks," she said, motioning to his redundant work. "You can set those right there," she said, pointing to the log.

Sometimes she had a way of making him feel so inept.

He dropped the kindling within her reach. She had her hands up, warming them.

"Where did you learn to do that?" he asked.

"Anyone worth their salt knows how to start a fire."

He raised a brow. He wasn't sure she was entirely right, but the comment intrigued him. She was definitely from a military family. Most people were vaguely curious about that kind of skill, but when it came to practical use, few had actually gone so far as to learn how to do it—especially in a wet environment.

"Did your dad teach you?"

"Are you asking me that because I'm a woman?"

"No." He sighed. "I'm asking because my dad taught me. When we came here for vacation, my dad loved to take us all out and spend time in the woods like this. When we got older, we were allowed to set our own camps, just so long as we were within yelling distance."

"Sorry, I didn't mean to be all defensive. It's just…"

"You're a feminist. There's nothing wrong with it. I can understand why you don't want to be underestimated."

"I don't know if I'd call myself a feminist or not. There are so many stigmas with that…but I do know that I'm tired of being put on a lower tier because I have ovaries."

He laughed, the sound echoing through the surrounding woods. "You are hilarious."

"There's nothing funny about being treated like you're not capable or that you should be subservient to a man. I think I should stand beside whomever is in my life, not behind him."

"That's not why I think you're hilarious," he said, picking up a log and moving it over by the fire so they could sit down together. "I guess *hilarious* is the wrong word. I just think you are amazing." He patted the spot next to him on the damp log. "I'd love to have you at my side."

She smiled, but it looked like she was trying not to. She sat down beside him. "You're not so bad yourself." She leaned against him, putting her head against his shoulder.

The action surprised him. He could make out the smell of the horse on her skin and the floral aroma that perfumed her hair, and the effect was perfect— a woman and a warrior.

"What about you?" she asked.

"Huh?" He tried to sit still, not quite sure if he should let her simply lean against him or if he should make a move and put his arm around her. The last time it hadn't ended so well.

It wouldn't be to his advantage if he made a

move and it resulted in them riding back in silence. It would be one heck of a long ride.

"Were you really in the military?"

"Uh." His body went rigid. She had just given him a speech about opening up and being honest, but he wasn't ready for her to start asking questions. "I was in the army."

"So you were toying with me about Schofield being a marine base?"

He gave her a guilty smile. "Maybe a little?" He tried to sound cute and semi-repentant.

"I see. Okay." She nodded. "When did you get out?"

He shook his head. "I've been out for about eight years. I only did a four-year tour—that was more than enough time."

"What didn't you like?"

He didn't want to answer that question. Something about it was so private. It was like in telling her, it would bare some of his soul. And yet… "I loved the travel, but I found that it was too *political* for my liking." He thought of all the times he had traveled in order to fulfill contracts and take out foreign leaders.

She was quiet for a long time. He leaned over and put the log on the fire.

"Chad didn't send hot dogs with you, did he?" she asked with a chuckle.

The reminder of food made his stomach rumble. Though he wanted to sit there forever with her, he got up and grabbed his go bag. Coming back, he dug through it. "Here, I've got a granola bar. And there's vodka." He pulled out a silver flask.

"Vodka?" She laughed. "That sounds like the meal of champions."

"The granola bar is complex carbs. The vodka—aside from being the beverage of the gods—is great for medical purposes as well as for relaxing." He tried to sound serious, but his voice was flecked with playfulness.

"I see. In case we needed to get drunk and eat carbs, we're totally covered. You don't have a steak in there, do you?"

"I wish." He laughed as he sat down beside her and she put her head back on his shoulder.

Handing her the flask and a bar, she took them and then opened the canteen's cap and took a long swig. As she handed it back, he followed suit. The vodka burned on the way down. He wasn't much of a drinker, but being this close to her it felt like it was called for. Maybe, for once, he could just relax around her.

They munched on their bars and he threw the wrappers into the fire, watching as they melted into nothing. It could have been the alcohol, but he was mesmerized by the flames as they danced. They were so beautiful, and he was reminded of the fleeting nature of it…and the life that succumbed to its force. In a way, Sabrina reminded him of the flames. She was so wild, free and alluring. He could have happily gotten lost in her for hours.

She reached over and into the breast pocket of his jacket, took out his flask and took another pull. Reaching back over, she slowly put it back, letting her fingers move over his chest. His body sprang to life, and as she touched him, he longed for more.

He took her cheek in his hand, caressing her fire-warmed skin. "I was serious when I said you are amazing. You...you are something special."

She looked at him and he watched the flames dance in her eyes. As their lips met, it was as if the entire world lit up around them.

IT WAS HAPPENING. Really happening. Sabrina couldn't remember exactly how they had gotten there. As his tongue caressed her bottom lip, she gave herself to the moment and decided not to dwell on it.

He held the back of her neck, his thumbs caressing her cheeks as they kissed. The world dissolved around her. The only thing existing was him, his lips, his warm touch on her cold face and the feel of his breath against her skin.

If she could, she would live in this moment forever.

Unfortunately, he pulled back, ending it far too soon. His cheeks were flushed, and there was a thin gleam of sweat on his skin even though it was bitterly cold.

"I…we…" she stammered, trying to be logical about what had just transpired between them, but all she could think about was how she wanted more—so much more.

Instead of saying anything, he reached into his go bag and pulled out a hatchet.

"Uh," she said, looking at the gleaming blade. "I didn't think the kiss was that bad. In fact, I was hoping you'd want to do it again."

He laughed as he put the blade behind his back and out of sight. "Crap, sorry! That's not it… I was just going to build us a little shelter."

"We kiss and you think *shelter*?"

He was such a dude. There she was thinking about feelings, and he was thinking survival.

Apparently, her kiss didn't carry the same magic it once had. In the past her kiss would have left a man thinking about nothing more than wanting the rest of her.

"I promise you…that's not it." He pulled his coat down a bit, covering his crotch. *Oh.*

Maybe she had a gift after all.

"You don't need to be embarrassed. I take that as a compliment." She gave him a coy look.

He laugh nervously. "Oh, believe me, I'm not embarrassed about anything I've got going on down there."

"Oh my goodness…" She laughed so hard her stomach hurt.

"If I have my way, you will see exactly what I mean."

"You have no shame, do you?"

He reached out and took her hand, giving it a squeeze. "Actually, I was thinking I'd build us a shelter so we could…get a bit more comfortable." He looked up at the sky where there were stars peeking through the dusk. "It's getting dark. Even if we turn around and start making our way back to the truck, we're going to be packing out in the dark. Our horse skills being what they are, I think it's best if we just wait out the night."

"That's the only reason you want to stay out here?" she asked, raising her brow.

"I have to take care of my lady first, then we can have the rest of the night to see where things go." He kissed her hand. "If you want, there's a couple of Mylar survival blankets in the bag. We can start setting up the lean-to." He started to say something else, but stopped. From the guilty look on his face, she could tell he'd been about to start giving orders.

He was learning that she didn't appreciate being told what to do. And the realization made her like him that much more. It was a rare man who wasn't intimidated by an independent woman.

"Don't go too far. If the Cusslers are close they'll come to investigate the fire," she said, looking into the shadows that surrounded them.

"I guess we'll need a door for our lean-to if we want our privacy."

The way he spoke sounded like he was joking, but she liked the idea. The last thing she wanted was to be spied on by a group of hillbillies in the middle of the night. Especially if things went to the place she wanted them to go with Trevor. She'd like to see exactly what he had been trying to cover with his coat.

They collected a few poles and set up a frame for their shelter. Trevor chopped off fresh boughs from the surrounding pines and, using them for the insulating materials, set them around the frame and on top to stop the snow from getting through. It didn't take long, but by the time they were done, she was starving. The granola bar had done little to keep the pangs of hunger at bay, but she could make it a day or two without food.

She sat down on the log by the fire and opened his bag. At the top was a handgun. The black steel immediately reminded her of why she was there in the first place, and all that hinged on her investigation of Trevor and his family.

If they had sex, it would compromise her in an entirely new way. If she did it, would be she doing it because she wanted to, or would there be a part of her that had sunk so low that she was willing to use her body to get ahead?

She hated the thought.

She pushed the gun aside and pulled out the Mylar

blankets. Opening the crinkling, tinfoil-like material, she set the first sheet on the pile of soft boughs that would act as their bed for the night. If this was what they were going to sleep on, it was going to make for a loud night.

Trevor came over and took the second blanket from her. Using a bit of duct tape, he lined the top of the shelter with the Mylar sheet so the fire's heat would be reflected down on them as they slept. As he worked, she could make out the scent of saddle leather and sweat and the sweet aroma of campfire on him. She'd never thought she was the kind of woman who would find that to be an aphrodisiac, but it was just that…especially when a bead of sweat worked its way down his temple, slipping into the corner of his lips.

She wanted to take those lips again. Thankfully, one of the horses chuffed. Getting up, Trevor followed suit, and they made their way over and readied them for the night.

As they finished, Trevor put his hands on his hips and stood admiring their work. Darkness had settled in on them, and with it came a whisper of tiredness. It had been a long, exhausting day, but she wasn't going to let it stand in the way…*if* she decided to act on her baser instincts.

She slipped her hand between his; her fingers were icy in comparison. "What, no door?" she teased, looking at their shabby-chic survivalist paradise.

"Well, I was thinking something in a teak... maybe mahogany." He let go of her hand and gave her butt a playful pat. "You are freaking funny, aren't you?" There was a brilliance in his eyes as he looked at her that made him appear even more handsome.

She had found herself an Adonis. Yeah, Mike had definitely set her up to take this fall.

But she was no Aphrodite and she couldn't fall in love with this ill-fated man. However, maybe just for one night, she could give in to her desires.

Stepping into the lean-to, she pulled him after her. The sheet crinkled under them as he lay down beside her. He unclicked his SIG Sauer P226 from his thigh and set it above their heads like an ominous reminder of the reality that awaited them when they stepped out of their silver wonderland. Wrapping her leg around his, she scooted into his nook and put her head on his chest. Maybe she could be satisfied with just this...the simple pleasure of lying in his arms.

Then again, there was something that seemed more dangerous about sinking into the comfort and safety of his arms...sex was intimate, but listening to the beat of his heart would be far more bonding. And that bond, the sacredness that came with letting someone into her heart, terrified her.

He ran his fingers through her hair. If she hadn't been so nervous, the sweet comfort of his touch would have put her to sleep. And yet all she could think of was where her hand rested on his abs. As he breathed, she could feel the muscles expand and contract. A warmth rose up from his core, growing steadily warmer as her hand eased down his stomach. She was so close to him. All it would take would be one little flip of the button and everything between them would change. For one night, he could be hers and she could be his…in every way.

One little button. How could she have let her future come to rest on one little brass button? She'd been playing this game long enough that she knew what she was setting herself up for; she couldn't claim ignorance now. And yet she was still surprised how *authentic* it felt being with Trevor. If she was just *her* and he was just, well, *him*, they could have made the world theirs.

He cleared his throat and stopped playing with her hair as her hand moved down until her fingers grazed the rough fabric of his blue jeans. "Sabrina?"

She stopped moving and looked up at him, gently resting her chin on his chest. "What?" she asked coyly.

He gave a light nervous cough and didn't seem capable of continuing.

"Shhh," she said, pressing her finger to his lips.

He drew her finger into his mouth and gave it a playful nibble. Her thighs clenched at the pleasure of the slight pain. She withdrew her hand and rested her fingers on the fateful button. Reaching down, he stopped her for a moment.

"Are you sure you want to do this?" he asked, giving her a look that was a mixture of desire and concern.

She understood exactly how he must have been feeling, but at this moment logical thought was failing.

"I want you, Trevor. I've wanted you since the first moment I laid eyes on you." She moved atop him, straddling him as she flipped open the button and unzipped his jeans. She looked into his eyes. "What about you? Do you want me?"

"More than you can possibly know." He emitted a slight growl, running his hand over his face. "But you are going to be the death of me." He took hold of her hips and she ground against him.

She giggled, but at the back of her mind she questioned if he was right in his assumption—literally. She forced down the thoughts. Now wasn't the time to worry what would come of their forbidden relationship. Now was the time for pleasure.

Sitting up slightly, she wiggled down his pants. Standing over him, as much as she could in the enclosed space, she slipped off her pants and black panties and let them drop on the Mylar beside him. The fire reflected off the silver sheets around them, but the chill of the night pressed in against her nakedness.

He sat up, taking hold of her. His hands were warm against her ass. He gave her a wicked smile as he kissed the soft skin of her inner thigh. His lips were hot against her cold skin, and as he inched his kiss higher up her leg, she was sure he was hotter than the flames that danced on the Mylar.

She reached up as his tongue met her, and her hands brushed against the world of fire around her.

"Trevor," she gasped, as his fingers found her. "I need you. Please," she begged, running her fingers through his long hair.

He kissed her again, then took her hand and leaned back, leading her atop of him. She pulled him inside her and in one slow movement, he filled her. There was nothing more glorious than this night… *their* night. It would be one memory she would cherish for the rest of her life.

Chapter Eight

The sun was breaking through the trees, but as they rode deeper into the backcountry, all Trevor could think about was the taste of Sabrina. He sucked at his bottom lip. He'd never known a woman could taste exactly like peaches.

And the face she had made when he'd pressed inside her. Just the thought made his body spring to life. Dang, he would give just about anything to be back in that lean-to, holding her against his chest and listening to the sounds she made when she was satisfied.

Ever since they'd loaded up and hit the trail this morning, she had been quiet. If she was like him, it was lack of sleep catching up with her, but it still surprised him. Not that he'd ever done this kind of thing before, but when he had slept with women in the past, normally the next day they opened up and wanted to talk. Sabrina was certainly a different kind of woman, and she definitely kept him on his toes. It was one of the things he loved about her—she challenged him.

As they rode up onto the top of the saddle that bridged two mountains together, in the distance he could make out a muddy game trail. Thanks to the pristine snow around it, the muddy mess looked like a snake slithering through an Arctic playground. The trail had probably been made by deer and elk, but it seemed out of place in the high country.

While animals were sometimes at the top of the mountains this time of year, it seemed like they would have moved lower to wait out the cold snap. Unlike humans, they heeded nature's warnings.

If he and Sabrina had been smart, they would've never spent the night up in the woods. It had been an ill-advised decision. Even without the possible ramifications of sleeping together, the weather alone could have been extremely dangerous. Luckily the storm hadn't been that bad, but if it had, they could have been stuck out in the wilderness for days. Even now there was no guarantee they would make it back unscathed.

The cold air nibbled at his nose as they rode toward the serpentine game trail. The distinct odor of campfire drifted toward him on the gentle breeze. "Do you smell that?" he asked, unsure if it was his clothing that he was smelling or if it came from some unknown source.

"Smoke." She looked around, pointing toward the east. "Look over there."

There was a fine tendril of wispy smoke drifting up and over the edge of the mountain. They were close to someone. But in the millions of acres that spread around them, it was impossible to know exactly who awaited them. Hopefully it was the Cusslers, and they could finally start making heads or tails of the situation they found themselves in. Then again, it might also be the second hillbilly family. Either way, they could be walking straight into a trap.

The people who lived in this kind of environment weren't stupid about survival. If they had any indication that he and Sabrina were coming up the mountain to find them, they wouldn't have built such a visible fire. In the event it was an ambush, they were ill-equipped to succeed.

Or at least one of them was.

He'd fought this kind of battle more times than he could count. It always seemed like the odds were stacked against him when it came to looking at something like this on paper, but his training and his level of expertise always gave him an advantage. They just had to play it smart.

He motioned for Sabrina to stop, riding up alongside her and climbing down off his horse. To their left was a small drop-off. He led his horse down the embankment and into the small stand of timber. Sabrina followed suit. They tied up their horses and he grabbed the go bag. Pulling out the gun, he handed it to her.

"You need me to explain how to use it?" he teased.

She smiled at him, but there was a sassy look on her face. "Isn't someone feeling feisty this morning?"

"That's not the only thing I'm feeling," he said, pulling her close and pressing his lips to hers. She wrapped her arms around his neck and dug her fingers into his hair, making him nearly groan.

"Hey now," she said, pulling back from him. "This isn't the time or the place for fooling around."

He didn't want to point out that last night was just as questionable, so he stayed quiet. She slipped the gun in the back of her pants and covered it with her jacket. There was something about the way she moved that made it look like she had done that a million times before. There was no hesitation, no shock at the feel of the cold steel against her skin and no second-guessing herself before she put the gun away. She was some kind of housekeeper.

"How accurate are you thinking you can be with that gun, if it comes down to it?" he asked.

"Let's just say starting a fire and working a truck and trailer weren't the only things my daddy taught me to do," she said. "If I were you, I would make sure I wasn't the one standing on the other end of my barrel."

He laughed quietly, looking over toward the

smoke as he realized that up here, with as little cover as they had, it also meant that sound would most certainly carry.

His phone buzzed in his back pocket. They must have found a tiny service signal. Moving to take it out and check, he stopped himself. "I need to take a whiz before we get started. Do you mind waiting here?"

"No problem," she said, waving him off.

It wasn't a great excuse, or charming, but it was the only thing he could think of to be alone for a few minutes.

He walked away from her and sat down behind a small knob on the hill where he couldn't be seen from above or below. Taking his phone out, he looked down at the screen. Chad had texted at least twenty times. Zoey had set up the fake drop in Seattle. They'd have at least a dozen eyes watching the place; if there was even a chance Sabrina wasn't who she said she was, he'd know.

Saying a silent prayer that he was wrong, he stuffed the phone back into his pocket. Last night had been inimitable, but he would love to try again.

But if Sabrina were working for some foreign government or the Gray Wolves, what had occurred between them would never happen again. More likely than not, his family would require that he take care of the problem. He couldn't stand the thought of hurting her.

He sat with his knees up, and he pressed his forehead against them as he closed his eyes. The cold snow was starting to melt and leach into his pants, making his butt cold, but he ignored the feeling. The biting cold was nothing compared to the gnawing he felt in his chest.

Hopefully he hadn't misplaced his trust when he'd put it with her.

For now, he could rest in the naive hope that he had found the one woman in this world to whom he could truly give his heart.

MEN. SOMETIMES THEY were so uncouth…it was like she was back in the good old boys' club that was a FBI resident agency.

As he walked away, she made her way down the embankment from the horses and found a little bush. As she unbuttoned her pants, her phone buzzed from inside her breast pocket. The sensation caught her completely off guard. She hadn't had service in the last day and it was a surprise that she even had any battery left, considering her phone had likely been searching for a signal since then. She pulled out her mobile, and looking over her shoulder to make sure Trevor was nowhere in sight, she punched in the code to unlock it.

Front and center in her inbox was an email from Mike. She opened it, and as she read, excitement and then a sense of dread filled her. Her team had intercepted an email sent from the Widow Maker. Apparently, Trevor and his team were supposed to make a drop in Seattle at seven tomorrow night. Mike wanted to know whether or not they were to move on the information.

She stopped reading and pressed the phone to her chest.

If that were true, then it was likely the reason Trevor had been only too happy to spend the night out in the woods. He'd probably wanted them to spend the night out here again so she was completely out of the equation. Maybe he still saw her as a security risk and wanted her as far from his dealings as possible. Then again, she hadn't given him any concrete reason, that she knew of, for him not to trust her. Besides, he would have to be at a meeting like that, wouldn't he?

She glanced back in the direction he had gone, but he was nowhere in sight.

Maybe Chad and the rest of the family were taking the lead on this one.

If the intelligence was legit, she needed to have a team there. Between the email and what they could glean from the handoff, her team would likely have more than enough for whatever prosecutor was put on their case. They could take down the family and put an end to their illegal gun trafficking once and for all. Then she could move on to another UC position. Maybe she could even get transferred away from Mike. She'd heard of some of her people taking remote location gigs; maybe she could get a little sunshine in and see the beaches of Colombia.

Going back to her phone, she told them to move on the intel.

If she was wrong, and Trevor or someone from his family had planted this for them to go on some wild-goose chase, her job would be on the line. The Bureau hated spending money and resources on anything that proved to be a dead end, but her gut was telling her that this was something they had to do. If she didn't act, and the Martins were in motion for a trade, then she'd miss her opportunity. Maybe it was a bit aggressive to jump on their first big break in the case, but if they could one-and-done this, she could go back to the agency with her head held high. Mike would have his deadline met and she would be the resident hero.

Besides, Trevor had probably set all this up... he'd brought her all the way to the backside of the moon knowing they were unlikely to have any digital reach. If he thought she was a threat, it was one heck of a plan. She'd been completely at his mercy. Why had she been so stupid in letting him take her on this ridiculous trail ride? She should have trusted her gut and found a way to stay behind. If he had gone without her, she could have been right there and dug deeper into the lead the IT crew had picked up. As it was, she might as well have been sitting on her hands.

She stuffed the phone back in her jacket and after doing her business, careful to keep the gun from falling in the snow, she made her way back to the horses. Trevor was already there, waiting for her. He had a worried expression on his face and after what she'd just learned, all she could do was stare at him. He was probably thinking about the deal he was going to miss.

The last thing she should have done was sleep with him. Heck, he'd probably even had that planned, too. Be cute, joke a bit, tell her she was beautiful, and she had turned to putty in his hands.

Why was she so stupid sometimes? She knew better than to let herself fall for a man like him.

She stretched, as if by doing so, she could wedge herself back into the box that was her role as a UC for the Bureau. There was a job to do. If she didn't think about the way his lips felt against her skin, or the way he sighed when he fell asleep, it wouldn't bother her too much.

He turned away from her and as he moved, there was a dark blue patch on his ass like he'd wet his pants. "You know," she teased, trying to relieve some of the stress that filled her, "most people take their pants down when they use the restroom."

"Oh…yeah…" He dropped his hands to the back of his jeans and gave a constricted laugh. "I slipped and fell down in the snow when I was trying to find a place. Nothing like a cold, chapped ass to remind you how good life is back at home." As he said the word *home*, his face pinched like there was something painful about the word itself.

She couldn't help but wonder if he really meant how good life was back where he could run guns once again.

She set her jaw. He was a killer. He put guns into the wrong hands, hands that were more than happy to pull the trigger even when the guns were pointed at the innocent.

He could act as endearing as he liked, but that didn't make him any less guilty.

She just had to remember not to be a fool—no matter how tempted she was to take on the enticing role as the woman on his arm.

No doubt he had one incredible, fast-paced and thrilling life. If only it was on the right side of the law.

Chapter Nine

She was acting weird. Or maybe he was, he couldn't decide. As they hiked toward the smoke, he couldn't make heads or tails of his thoughts. This was all driving him mad. At least he would soon find out one way or another if she could be trusted. He would have his answer and then they could move forward—or not.

The snow crunched under their feet, the sound reminding him of what needed to be done. All they had to do was get to the bottom of the Cussler brother's death for now. He could deal with the rest when he got home.

Yes, shoving the thoughts of her possible deception away...yes, that was the best answer. If he was acting weird, at least he could put an end to it this way and slide back into his role as one of the Martin brothers—tech billionaires extraordinaire, complete with a fictionalized military backstory...well, sort of fictionalized. Some of his experiences with the military had been all too real.

That's all this feeling was, his past coming back to haunt him. He was out of that game. Now he just had to look to the future.

If only it were that simple.

Becoming a civilian was proving to be far harder than he had expected it to be. He'd always thought that the people who had the biggest issues were also the ones whose egos wouldn't allow them to step away from the game. He'd never thought that *he* would be one of those people. Sure, his identity had been all spook all the time, but that wasn't who he *was*. He had always thought of himself as so much more…and yet he was constantly proving himself wrong. Even the way he made his bed every day spoke of his passion for a life that was no longer going to be his once he retired completely.

There was a click and slide in the distance, just like the sound of a round being jacked into a bolt-action rifle. He glanced in the direction of the smoke. They had to be at least a half mile away from the possible camp. They were surrounded by a blanket of white, interspersed with dots and jags of gray and black and trees that had fallen victim to a recent forest fire. In the world of white, nothing moved. Yet the sound had been nearly unmistakable.

He'd heard that grind of metal too many times in his life to get it wrong.

"Get down," he said, moving behind a piece of deadfall and motioning toward Sabrina to follow suit.

She looked at him like he had lost his mind, but she did as he told her and squatted down beside him. "What is it? Did you see something?" she whispered.

As the last syllable fell from her lips, a bullet whistled by them. Without thinking, he pushed Sabrina all the way to the ground so she was lying behind the log. Based on the sound and the percussive wave of the shot, whoever was shooting at them was uphill, not far. He knelt as low as he could, using the tree for as much cover as possible. He pulled his phone and using the selfie angle, he looked behind him.

At the top of the trail, he could make out the black tip of a rifle barrel.

They couldn't move. If they dared to go anywhere they would be an easy target for whoever was holding that gun. Their adversary literally had the upper hand.

"Can you see who it is?" Sabrina asked.

"Can't see their face, but whoever it is, they are using a high-caliber rifle. Any closer, and a tree just might not be wide enough to keep us safe." He moved to pull his SIG Sauer out of his thigh holster, but then he realized it was already in his hand. He had no idea when he had taken the gun out, and yet he was impressed by his body's autonomous reaction to gunfire.

Maybe being a trained mercenary really did have its advantages after all.

"Take out your—" Before he could say the word *gun* he noticed that, just like him, she had her weapon drawn and ready. The gun was pulled close to her chest and high, the position of a law enforcement officer or a well-trained marksman.

She had said she'd been trained to use weapons by her father, but she didn't appear to be a Sunday shooter.

She rolled and moved to look over the log. As she readjusted, another round pinged through the air. This time, it sounded like it struck something to their left.

"Do you think they're really that bad a shot?" he asked. "Or are they messing with us?" The question was as much a legitimate question as it was a test for her.

She looked up the hill, like she was gauging the distance. "The gun's caliber is too big to be using open sights—they have to have a scope on it. And if they have a scope on it, they could hit the hair on a gnat's ass at this range. They have to be messing with us. Either they're trying to flush us out, or they're sending us a message that we aren't welcome."

Test failed. She was definitely no Sunday shooter.

"You're right," he said, crestfallen. "Which leaves us with two options. We can fight—and turn this into a shooting gallery—or we can sit here and wait for them to get bored and leave. But if we wait, and they really are out to kill us, then they may well get the drop on us and move around until they have a better angle. We could be sitting ducks."

In a way, regardless of what the person shooting at them chose to do, he couldn't help feeling like he was a sitting duck with Sabrina. It seemed all too likely that she wasn't the woman she was pretending to be. Hell, she probably had gotten pinged on her phone the second he'd gotten pinged on his. Maybe she had heard something that had turned her off of him… Maybe she was already making plans for the fake drop in Seattle. That would explain why she was acting so weird.

He grumbled aloud. He couldn't fall back down that chasm, no. No more second-guessing himself. No more second-guessing her.

He had bigger things to worry about right now. He was being ridiculous by allowing his mind to wander. He had to focus.

The wind kicked up as quarter-size snowflakes cascaded down from the sky, making the entire world look like something inside a snow globe. It was his chance. Though they only had small arms, he'd have to make a break for it.

"Cover my six," he said, moving his chin in the direction of the shooter.

"Are you crazy?" Sabrina asked. "If you go out there, you'll be an open target."

She wasn't wrong; there was little cover. "That's what you're here for," he said, smiling in an attempt to downplay the danger they were in and put her mind at ease. "You're going to have to put your money where your mouth is. You said you're good marksman."

"I didn't mean I was *this* good. They have to be at least fifty yards away—way outside my comfort zone." She grabbed his hand, stopping him from moving. "Don't go." There was a deep well of concern in her eyes.

He had to act for the same reason she didn't want him to go—he had to shield her, the woman he loved.

Not that she could ever know that.

Though if she thought about it, she'd probably quickly realize that he wasn't the kind of man who would risk his life for just anyone.

He moved his hand out of hers and snapped a round into the chamber of his weapon. "Start shooting in three…two…" He stood up and raced up the hill, firing as he zigzagged haphazardly over downed trees and rocks. The brush pulled at his feet, threatening to bring him to his knees and welcome him to his death.

Taking a hard right, he watched as the gunman's barrel came into view above him. He hit the ground as the muzzle flashed. The bullet thumped as it ripped into the tree base just inches from his head.

Gunfire rang out from Sabrina's direction. There

were twenty-two rounds in each of his guns' magazines. They'd have to be smart about this.

As Sabrina fired, he jumped back to his feet. A couple dozen yards in front of him was a large boulder. It was a long way to go without cover, but he had to go for it. He sprinted as hard as he could up the hill. The shooter fired. The bullet pinged off a rock, ricocheting into the air.

He slumped down behind the boulder. His breath came in heavy gasps, but he barely noticed as adrenaline coursed through him. Sabrina was out of sight, tucked behind the deadfall. *Good.*

For a moment, the world was silent. Fat blobs of snow coursed down, one landing on his nose and quickly melting, like some warning to him about the impermanence and fickle nature of life. He needed no reminder.

Trish flashed into his mind. She would have loved this. There was nothing she jonesed for quite like a good firefight. She was probably looking down on him from heaven. The thought came with an ethereal bit of warmth.

He smiled up at the sky, knowing full well that it was probably nothing more than his mind playing tricks on him, but he didn't care. If there was even a tiny chance she was here with him now, he needed her to know he loved and missed her. Maybe he could even make things right by saving Sabrina now.

Raising his gun, he charged from behind the rock

and ascended the hill. He expected gunfire to rain down on him, but as he ran there was nothing except the crunch of his boots in the snow. As he breached the crown of the mountain, he stopped. There was no one there. A little way down from where he stood was a stand of timber, thick and dense as it had somehow escaped the ravaging effects of the fire that had taken down its sister side.

Near him on the ground was the packed snow where someone had been lying down. A smattering of brass casings littered the ground. From the patch of packed snow, there was a set of tracks leading into the timber and then they disappeared between the trees. The shooter was probably watching him right now. The hairs on the back of his neck stood up as he realized how easily the shooter could set up again from behind a tree and take an open shot at him.

He moved to the patch of boulders they had been using as coverage. Whoever had been shooting must have planned out this location. In defense and offense it was literally perfect—high point, great coverage and the ability to blend in with the background. He couldn't have done a better job himself.

Whistling down, he motioned over the hillside for Sabrina. She stood up and he waved her forward, surveilling the area around her as she hiked up the steep hillside. His breath made a cloud in the air as he guarded her and the cold bore down upon them.

It was colder up here, even more frigid than it had been the night before.

They'd gone a whole day without food and the water supply was running low; soon they'd have to start thinking about boiling snow. They couldn't afford to chase after whoever it was that had been trying to gun them down, but they were so close. They couldn't stop now.

Sabrina plopped down beside him, her breathing heavy. "Holy crap, that hill didn't look that steep from the bottom. How did you run up it?"

He chuckled. "Someone taking aim at you tends to give you an extra incentive to move."

"You're hilarious," she said sarcastically, nudging his arm as she slipped her gun back into the waistband of her pants. "I don't see any blood."

"And I haven't seen anyone moving. Either they are hunkered down somewhere in that timber—" he motioned toward the stand down the hill "—or they hightailed it out of here."

She motioned toward the curl of smoke rising up from the center of the timber. "Do you think we have enough rounds to go down there, poke around and see if we can flush anyone out?"

"I can't put you in danger. At least not more danger than we're already in—up here, in the middle of nowhere, if one of us gets hurt, we may never make it out."

"From the moment we left the ranch, we've both

known that this was a high-risk situation." She moved closer to him and put her hand on his knee. "Even when things are hard, I'm not one who gives up."

"But this isn't a battle of wills, or resilience." He put his hand atop hers and traced the length of her finger with his. "This is possibly life or death, and I don't want anything to happen to you."

She gazed into his eyes, and as she looked at him he could see the start of tears. And yet the look on her face wasn't happiness; it was like she was torn. Maybe she was feeling just as confused as he was about this entire situation and how unlikely it seemed that they would end up together.

"Trevor, you…*we* are amazing. I know I shouldn't say this, but I've never met anyone like you. I don't know what it is about you, but even now just sitting here close to you, with bullets raining down on us at any minute… I dunno why, but I feel safe. More than that, I would be the happiest woman alive if I could stay out here and avoid going back to the real world if it meant I could spend another second with you." The expression on her face seemed to darken as she spoke, in contrast to what she was telling him.

"But?" He waited for the ax to fall.

She huffed. "But…" She paused, suddenly taken with her pants' stitches. "But I don't think we should be worried about it right now."

That wasn't what he was expecting her to say.

He'd assumed she was going to tell him she wanted nothing to do with him once they got out of the woods, that she was quitting the ranch, or she had some deep dark secret that would keep them from coming together, but not this. As much as her avoidance was a relief, it was going to nag at him. There was something she wasn't saying, that she must not be ready to tell him. And yet he had to respect her needs and not push her to open up more than she was comfortable with.

She reached down in the snow beside them, digging in the white fluff like a nervous tic. Her fingers reddened as she moved them around in the snow, and it melted and stuck to her skin. Even though it was not his own hand, he could feel the sting of the cold, and he wanted to take her fingers and warm them for her so she wouldn't feel any pain. But he stopped himself. It seemed like perhaps he wasn't what she wanted.

She gasped, pulling her hand from its icy diversion. In her grasp was a spent casing. She flipped it over, reading the caliber stamped into its base.

"This came from an HK416," she said, staring at the brass in her hand.

There was no way she could possibly know about the Heckler & Koch assault rifle. It wasn't a particularly common gun, though they could be bought on the black market. "What do you mean? How do you know?" The knot in his stomach returned, larger than ever.

"This brass is nearly identical to a .223, but here." She handed the casing over. "If you feel the weight, it's significantly lighter."

He took the casing and rolled it around in his hand, but he wasn't thinking about the cold metal thing; rather, who the stranger was sitting next to him. He stuffed the round in his pocket and stood up.

"Why would it be lighter?" he asked, even though he already knew the answer.

"In 2012, the army commissioned manufactures to reduce the weight of the brass casings in this type of round by 10 percent. That means that this weapon most likely belongs to someone who is either active military or FBI." As she looked up at him and their gazes met, her expression changed from focused to guilty.

"Sabrina." He said her name like it was just as much of a secret as whatever she was hiding from him. "Tell me the truth. Who sent you?"

Chapter Ten

She had screwed up, royally. Her hubris had caught up with her and she had no one to blame but herself. Why did she have to open her stupid mouth?

Her investigation was over. She was done. Her cover was blown.

Sure, she could lie about why she was here, but even if he pretended to believe her he would never really trust her again. And if she came out with the truth, he'd inevitably run her out of his life like the infiltrator she was.

But she had to try to cover her ass and buy more time with him. Maybe she could salvage something from this investigation—maybe even clear his name and keep his family out of federal prison.

He opened his hand and helped her stand. "Just tell me." There was a deep sadness in his voice, and it broke her heart.

It hurt more than she ever would have expected. This wasn't her first investigation to go off the rails, but it had never happened like this before. In this moment, it was her life—her *real* life—that was most impacted.

If she told him the truth, maybe they could work together and come through this—but that seemed like one heck of a pipe dream. To hope for something like that was like having faith in humanity—a great philosophy, but rarely worked in practice.

She had been sent here to stop him from putting weapons into the enemy's hands, and yet as the minutes slipped by it was like her objectivity had collapsed. Her heart had come into play and she hated it.

"Trevor, I want everything to work out for everyone involved." She reached over and cupped his face in her hands. "None of this is what I expected when I came to the Widow Maker Ranch. I'm hopeful everything is going to play out all right, but I need you to tell me some things."

He nodded but remained stoic. "Is your name even Sabrina?"

She huffed. Of course he'd be questioning her from the ground up. If she was in his shoes she would be doing exactly the same thing. "Yes."

"And what happened last night… Were you just playing me?"

She stepped closer to him, their bodies brushing against each other. She ran her hand down his neck and rested it on his shoulder. "I'm not the kind of woman who jumps into bed with a man. Ever. There has to be something there, really there, before I'll even consider being intimate."

His lips pursed and he nodded, remaining silent. Stepping away from her touch, he turned around and slowly made his way toward the smoke rising up from the stand of timber. His hands were limp at his sides, and the gun nearly dangled from his fingers.

He was in shock, hurt and probably analyzing exactly how this was going to play out. She had admitted nothing, at least not directly, but he had to realize what a liability she was for him and his family. He made it clear from the very beginning that his family was the most important thing to him, and she had no doubt he was willing to do whatever it took to keep them safe. And that placed her in more danger than when an unknown gunman had taken aim at her. At any moment, Trevor could decide to take her out.

It was unlikely anyone would ever find her remains if he chose to kill her.

She started walking after him, following his footsteps in the snow. The trees moved in on her like brooding sentinels, as if they, too, were judging her for the role she had taken on with the Martin family. Trevor, more than anyone, should've understood what it meant to do a job like hers. He had a life filled with secrets as well. Secrets that she still wasn't privy to. And yet those same secrets could save them.

Trevor was growing ever more distant, and the

shadows of the timber threatened to help him disappear. Right now, that was probably exactly what he wanted to do. In fact, it was almost exactly what she wanted to do as well. However, she didn't want to lose him. She wanted to keep on living this fictional life—a life in which she was free to love and she could put aside the possibility that he was her enemy.

"Trevor," she called after him.

He turned and waited for her to catch up. As she neared, she could have sworn there were faint marks on his cheeks where tears had fallen, but she hated to think she had elicited such a response from him— the warrior.

"Don't say anything." He raised his hand. "I need some time to work through all of this."

She nodded. "I'm serious, just know that I want to help you. We can be on the same side."

He turned away from her and kept walking; the subtle evasion amplified her pain. They walked in silence until they came upon a small clearing. At its center was a dying campfire. There was a collection of pots and pans, mugs, and blue plates. It looked as though at least five people had struck camp and had been eating breakfast when they suddenly fled.

The footsteps in the snow went off in all directions. If they followed each trail, they would be tracking for hours.

Trevor walked to the right, moving around the fire as he searched the ground. She made her way left, as she tried to focus on the work at hand instead of the conversation that Trevor didn't want to have.

Not far from the back side of the camp there was a smattering of blood upon the snow.

"Trevor, can you look at this?" She pointed at the ground.

He made his way over. A faint smile played across his lips. "Looks like we may have hit the shooter after all."

"Maybe we don't make such a bad team," she said, but the sentiment came out sounding more like a question.

He didn't respond, squatting down beside the bloodied snow. "This is definitely fresh. It's still melting. But based on the little amount of blood, I'm thinking we just winged him—or her."

"If we did hit one of them, they're going to be moving slow." She looked out into the timber. "We could probably catch up to them if we move fast."

Trevor sighed as he stood up. "Nah, I think we should head back." He brushed by her as he looked around the camp.

She should have been following suit, looking around to see if they could find anything to give them a clue about who had been shooting at them, but all she could focus on was Trevor.

The second they got out of the woods and headed back to the ranch everything would be completely over—her investigation, the case, her job and their relationship. But she couldn't blame him for wanting to get out of the woods and away from her.

They walked around the timber near the deserted camp for a bit longer, but time seemed to lose any reference. She kept looking to him, hoping the right words would find her, but none came. Between them there was only awkward silence smattered with unspoken feelings.

It felt like a breakup, even though there was nothing formal to end.

Maybe this kind of work, as a UC, wasn't something she was cut out for. Normally she was fine, but her emotions had never come into play. If she couldn't keep her heart out of her work, she had no business doing it.

She'd have to give Mike her notice as soon as she got back into service. Not to mention the fact that she'd have to tell them she had let them all down. Mike was going to have a field day with this. He'd always told her she was weak, and now it turned out that he was right.

Trevor finally stopped as they came back to the edge of the timber and to the camp. He looked in the direction of the shooter's perch. "How did you know about the HK416 being a FBI weapon? Is it because you're an agent?" He turned to face her, but from the emotionless look on his face she couldn't tell exactly what he wanted her to say.

A lump formed in her throat. She tried to swallow

it back and to replace her nervousness with bravery, but it didn't work. She was scared for so many reasons, the biggest being that if she walked away from Trevor, she would be walking away from the love of her life. The thought tore her apart.

"I…" She struggled to find the right thing to say. There was no easy way out of this. "Yes, I was sent here because of what happened in Turkey. We have reason to believe that you were responsible for several civilians' deaths… That, and a few other things."

He reached over and braced himself against a tree. The bark crumbled under his fingers, littering the ground with the ashy remnants of what had been so beautiful only moments before. Everything was disintegrating.

"So you came here believing that I was some kind of monster?" There was a pained look in his eyes.

"No, I came here to find out the truth. And the moment I met you, I knew that things weren't going to be as black-and-white as I'd hoped. You are nothing like the man I expected to meet." She wanted to reach out and touch him, to reassure him that everything was going to be okay—but the truth was, she didn't know whether everything would be all right or not.

"And you know about Trish's death?"

She nodded. "What happened to her…from what I know, it wasn't your fault."

He leaned against the tree, crossing his arms over

his chest. "You're only saying that to create a bond—empathize with your target, make them feel safe. I know your game."

His words tore at her, ripping away what little was left of her defenses. "I'm not playing a game. If I were, I'd never have told you the truth about me being an agent. Until very recently, I wasn't sure about you. But I've come to believe that you are incapable of hurting an innocent person." She couldn't stand it; she reached over and put her hand on his chest. His heart was thrashing beneath her touch. "Don't think I didn't notice that you weren't shooting earlier. You could've gone in there guns blazing, but you took the high road. That takes an entirely different level of bravery."

"That wasn't bravery, it was curiosity." He looked down at her hand but didn't move to take it. "I didn't want to kill the one person who could have possibly known about the Cussler brother's death. I have to know how close all my enemies really are." He moved away from her.

She'd broken the bond they'd had, irreparably.

"I know you probably don't believe me, but I'm not one of them. I have the power to condemn you—if I'd found evidence—and I also hold the power to clear your name. But I need to know some truths from you, something I can take back to my handler to prove that you're the man that I know you are—

and not the gunrunning terrorist the FBI believes you to be."

His indifferent expression changed to one of complete shock as he opened and closed his mouth like he was struggling to find the right words. "How much do you know about me?"

The way he asked made her wonder if she had missed some glaring detail.

She'd already admitted her truth to him, so all she could think of was the old adage *in for a penny, in for a pound*.

"I know that you and your family are in fact a group called STEALTH. You've been running guns around the globe for a number of years now. I know, and the FBI has proof, that you are involved in the trade. I don't know to what degree, and I'm hoping our intelligence was wrong—that you are just the little fish and we are going after the whales. From what I've seen, you don't seem like the type of man who would put guns into the hands of those who wish to do the most harm."

"You're right, I don't want to hurt anyone who doesn't deserve to be taken to their knees. But being in the FBI, you have to know as well as I do that there are truly wicked people out there. And the only way to bring those kinds of monsters down is to send monsters after them…and just like you first assumed, I am that monster." He sat down on a log next to the dying campfire.

She didn't know what to make of what he was saying. Was he admitting his crimes? If so she had no choice but to turn him over when they got back to the ranch. Perhaps that was what he wanted, to fall on the sword and go to prison…otherwise, why would he have so easily admitted to his mistakes? And yet there was something about the way he spoke that made her wonder if there was more to the story.

"Why, Trevor?" She sat down beside him.

"Why what?"

"Why do you think you're a monster?" She tented her fingers between her knees as she leaned forward and looked back at him.

"I had nothing to do with civilian deaths in Turkey. Yes, I took down my enemy combatants— I've killed. And if you asked me if I'd do it again, I wouldn't hesitate to say yes. Especially when it came to trying to save Trish. I'll do anything to save the people I love," he said, a deep sadness in his voice. "But I'm also the man who is willing to run into a burning building and save the innocent. I'm the man people call in the dead of night when the demons seep out of the cracks and wish to do them harm. So you can judge me however you wish. I'm guilty of plenty of things that society deems wrong, but in my heart, I know that I'm the man who is doing what many others can't. I make the hard choices."

She sat in silence, trying to come to terms with the things he was saying. He wasn't like any gun dealer she'd ever met before—not that she'd met many. He didn't seem to be after money or driven by greed. Instead he seemed almost like her, focused on humanitarian need and the prospect of justice—but in the most unconventional way. And she still didn't understand how giving guns to warlords was saving the innocent. Was this an elaborate rationalization?

"Trevor, why were you running guns?"

He smirked and ran his hands over his face. "That's past tense. We don't do it now. We got out of the game after everything with Trish. So if you think you're going to help the FBI and federal prosecutors by coming after my family, it's nonsensical. We're out of the game."

She didn't know whether or not to bring up Seattle. He was lying to her—they were still very much active in the trade—but she couldn't reveal everything she knew. Not if there was a chance he was playing her for a fool. "But you admit you have been putting guns into the wrong hands?"

"Just like you said *trust me*, now I ask the same of you. What I did, I did because I had to. Yes, the ethics were somewhat ambiguous, but there were greater things at play than even you know."

"What do you mean?"

"I mean that you don't have all the answers, and neither do I. But I'm not the bad guy here. Just like you, I do what I have to do—sometimes at the cost of others."

"You don't care that civilians are dying because of you?" The question came out and slashed like a sword. She hadn't meant it to be as harsh as it sounded, but she needed to know exactly where he stood. Both of their futures depended on it.

He shook his head. "I know it doesn't look like it from the outside, but I wanted to keep people safe just as much as you do. When I realized I couldn't, that's when I came here. If I can't even keep my own sister safe, then I have no business out there. Thinking I could make a difference, it's almost the definition of stupidity."

"You're not responsible for your sister's death. I've seen the reports. Maybe they didn't have all the facts, or the answers, but I saw the forensic analysis. From where you were standing, you could have never gotten there in time to help. The shooter had the advantage."

"You may have seen the science behind everything, but what you didn't see was someone you love looking up at you and knowing that they needed your help, and yet all you could do was watch them die."

She wanted to hold him and tell him it would be okay, that time would heal. And yet he wasn't hers. They were enemies, at least in his mind. If she even tried to console him, it would come off as false—and only drive them further apart.

She couldn't make his heart feel something toward her that his mind wouldn't allow.

And as much as she knew she shouldn't reach for him, she did. She took his hand in hers and lifted it to her face. "Trevor, I'm so sorry. For everything. For Trish. For this. For the investigation. But you're not alone in your suffering. When I was young, I lived in Redmond—"

"On a military base, or was that a lie, too?" he asked, pulling his hand away.

He had every right to snap at her. "Some of what I told you was backstory, but there is some truth to it. I find it easier to have an identity that I can actually relate to. My dad was in the military. He was controlling and passionate about his Second Amendment rights—until he and my mother were found in a parked car at the bottom of Mount Rainier, murdered. I was sixteen."

They sat there in silence for a long moment. "I'm sorry, Sabrina. I know how hard it can be to lose people you love." He turned to her. "Is your parents' murder the reason you decided to become involved in the Bureau?"

She nodded. "After their death, I had nowhere to go. I was shipped around foster homes in the area for a while until I ended up in a nice couple's house in Redmond. The guy worked for a local law firm and the woman worked at the federal office. My guardian set me up with an interview at the FBI after I graduated from college. Go Huskies," she said, raising her hand in the air in feigned excitement.

"Did they ever solve your parents' murder?" he asked.

She shook her head. "And the files are buried. I've tried to look into them a few times, but I don't have the clearance."

"It sounds like there's more to your parents' murder than the Bureau wants you to know."

She chuckled. "We live in a world full of conspiracy theories, don't we?"

"They're not always theories. Sometimes the most outrageous things I see and hear are the truth." He picked up one of the blue camp plates like he was inspecting the edges. "As much as you want to get to the bottom of your parents' murder, you probably need to let it go. You're chasing ghosts, and when you do that you open yourself up for a lifetime of disappointment. One ghost leads to another, which leads to another, and then all you end up with is heartbreak and a life haunted by questions you'll never have the answers to."

"Sounds like that's something you have a little bit of experience in," she said, looking into his eyes.

"I don't want to talk about it, but people don't lead lives like ours if they have a healthy childhood."

Trevor threw the plate he'd been holding and it hit the exposed ground opposite them with a clatter.

"Why did you do that? You know that had to echo throughout the entire forest." She motioned toward the plate.

"They wanted us to come here. They'll be glad to know we took the bait."

She looked around. From what she could see it looked like a regular old campsite. There were no booby traps or any other evidence that they'd been set up, so she wasn't sure where he was coming up with this idea.

Almost as if he could read her mind, he continued, "Did you notice everything around here is brand-new? If you look at our guy's tracks, his boot marks are still in perfect diamonds and squares. And that plate, and all the dishes, barely have any marks on them. And if you look at this makeshift camp, everything has been moved here within the last day or two." He pointed toward the ground. If they'd been here long, the ground would be trampled well beyond this.

"So what? Maybe they just got here. These people are travelers."

"If these are the Cusslers, or their enemies, they aren't the type to be running to Walmart to get cookware and boots very often. Either they aren't who we've been thinking they are, or we're chasing the wrong ghosts."

She couldn't think of anyone else who could have been behind this.

"While I have my fair share of enemies, they aren't people who would shoot at me and miss. The people who want to kill my family are the type who can kill from two miles away, like our friends in Turkey. Which means it's likely that whoever is behind this is after you. Who have you ticked off lately?"

No. He was grasping at straws. There was no way she was the target here. He couldn't turn this back on her. This was his mess. His family's drama. Not hers.

Unless everything wasn't on the up and up with Mike.

The brass they'd found, the new plates, the manic deadline and the threatening emails…the evidence wasn't in the Bureau's favor, but everything he was pointing out was circumstantial. Sure, she had enemies—who didn't? It didn't mean that anyone was after her.

And yet she had a sinking feeling Trevor was right.

Chapter Eleven

Trevor wasn't sure if he had assumed correctly or not but he could tell he had planted just enough doubt about her team to create a distraction. As soon as they got back, he would alert the family that they were under investigation. In just a couple of hours, they could bug out—and disappear once again. He'd always heard Crete was beautiful. He could use a little bit more of a tan, and he certainly wouldn't miss snow.

As they walked back to the horses, he tried not to feel guilty as he took in the view of her walking ahead of him. He would be lying if he didn't admit how much he enjoyed that picture. He loved the way her hips swung back and forth as she picked her way through the underbrush that led to the serpentine trail. He'd miss that almost as much as he'd miss feeling her breath on his skin when she fell asleep with her head on his chest. It had been a long time since he'd made love, but the things she had done with her hips were unlike anything he'd ever experienced before. He couldn't risk losing her.

If the situation had been different, she was definitely the kind of woman he could imagine settling down with. Then again, he was never planning to settle down again. Maybe she was more the kind of woman he could imagine traveling the world with. A scene from the movie *Tombstone* came to mind— with Wyatt and Josie slipping away into the sunset aboard a cruise liner and setting out on a life of adventure together.

But she was his adversary. She was trying to take down his family. Or at least she *had* been. It had to count for something that she had outed herself to him. Working with the CIA, he knew exactly how much was at risk in doing so—and exposing the truth to him may have put her job on the line. She certainly couldn't continue their investigation—but just because she left didn't mean that his family wouldn't still draw scrutiny from the Bureau. Just for once he wished he could call his friends in the CIA and have them whisper the truth into someone's ear in order to get this all to stop.

He'd end up dead long before the truth reached the right people. The Gray Wolves had their men everywhere, and where they didn't have their own people, they had paid informants. There was a lot of money to be made if a person was the type who was willing to sell state secrets.

"Sabrina, can you think of someone who wants you gone at the FBI?"

She stopped walking and turned around to face him. "There's always someone who is breathing down your neck behind closed doors."

The pinched expression on her face told him he had struck a nerve. She definitely had enemies.

"Is there anyone you can trust inside the Bureau?"

She looked off into the distance, as if she were contemplating her answer. "I know you think you're onto something, but I just don't see anyone working this hard to get me fired. If my enemies wanted to see me go, all they had to do is fudge a little paperwork."

"It isn't that easy. I *know* it isn't."

She quirked her eyebrow. "And how would you know? Did your family do an in-depth study of the Bureau?"

He chuckled. "You and your BuCrew aren't nearly as secret as you all would like to think you are. Sure, you have great people in tech, but when it comes to the truth I'm learning that you guys are at least ten steps behind."

"And yet we knew all about you and your family's dealings." She gave him a smart-ass tilt of the head.

If only she knew the truth, she wouldn't be so glib. And yet he could never reveal his truth to her. It wasn't just his to reveal.

"At least you can find some comfort in the fact that your enemies don't want you dead, or else they

are just crappy shots," he teased her. "If this is someone from the FBI taking potshots at us, with all your
long gun training through Quantico, I'm sure your
instructors would've been so proud." He laughed.
It felt good to be able to joke with her once again.

"Hey now, we don't know for sure whether or not
those were my people shooting at us. In fact, if those
were *my* people then I guess they weren't really mine
after all, were they?" she pondered aloud.

"You are ridiculously cute when you're being asi-
nine. You know just as well as I do that it was your
enemies up there—FBI or not."

"I just think it's too far-fetched. It seems more
likely that it's someone who wanted to make it look
like FBI or a government agency. Plenty of these off-
the-grid types are anti-government. It's easy enough
to get your hands on those types of weapons. You
know all about it." She gave him a judgmental look.

He walked up beside her and slipped his hand into
hers. "How about we put a bet on this? If we get to
the bottom of this and it's someone close to you, you
have to spend another night with me—we'll order
room service."

She gave him a playful grin. "Since you seem so
certain, if it ends up being someone involved with
your family—which by the way, seems far more
likely—then you owe me two things. One, you have
to keep my secret, under threat of penalty of death,
should you expose me."

He loved that she could threaten him with death and it turned him on. "And your second ask?"

"A favor yet to be named. Do we have a deal?"

"I don't make bets when I don't know what's at stake."

"It's a deal, or there's no deal at all." Her playful grin grew even more impish. "It all comes down to how much you believe in your theory."

She was calling him out—testing to see exactly what cards he had up his sleeve. "Okay, deal…but the second ask can't be for something I don't want to give."

"Again," she said, a look of pure innocence on her face as she cajoled him, "all or nothing."

"Then *all* it is." He didn't like the deal, but something deep in his gut told him that he was right and there was more to this than what they had first assumed.

The ride out of the woods took far less time than it had taken them to ride in. As they passed by their makeshift lean-to, he found himself once again wishing they could go back in time.

He wasn't angry at her admission of working for the FBI, not as he watched her ride in front of him. She had a job to do, just like he did. And the fact that she had finally admitted the truth to him went a long way. She certainly didn't have to do that. And it proved to him, more than anything else she could have done, that he could trust her. In a way, it also made him wonder if she was just as emotionally invested in what happened in that lean-to as he was—which meant, she must have realized how impossible their relationship would be.

If nothing else, at least they could walk away from each other knowing that somewhere in the world there was a person who really cared for them.

The ranch was dead quiet as they rode up with the truck and trailer. Unsaddling the horses, they barely spoke. It was as if she knew just as well as he did that things between them were about to come to an end.

There was no way they could go back and pretend they weren't the people they truly were, the people they had revealed to each other up on the mountain. If only he could have told her his truth as well, that he was working for the CIA, and yet…he couldn't. If he did, it would serve nothing. She would still have to leave, but when she did she would be in even more danger than when she arrived. The people he worked for weren't the kind who liked leaving loose ends. They made Trevor and his family look like teddy bears in comparison.

Instead of taking the horses straight back to Dunrovin Ranch, they'd decided to head home. It could have been all the riding or all the emotions he experienced over the last few days, but when they hit the front door, he was exhausted.

When he walked in, Chad was sitting on the couch, watching ESPN. He looked up and his expression darkened as though he could see from their faces that something was up.

"How'd it go? Did you find them?" Chad asked, flicking off the television.

Sabrina glanced over at Trevor. "Hey, I'm going to run out and unload the horses and put them in the barn. You guys go ahead and talk." She gave him a pleading look, as though she didn't want him to tell his brother what she had told him, but also understood he couldn't let a secret that big just stay between them.

He hated being in this position.

"Okay, I'll be right out and I can help you grab the rest of the stuff out of the truck." Stepping closer, he was going to give her a quick peck to the forehead, and then stopped himself. Chad didn't need more fodder for the fight they were likely about to have.

As the door closed behind Sabrina, Trevor walked over and sat down on the couch beside his brother. His knees ached from all the riding, making him feel old and tired.

Chad leaned forward looking him in the eye. "Are you going to tell me what that was all about?"

And so it began.

He couldn't look his brother in the eye, and he wished Chad hadn't turned off ESPN—it would've made things easier.

"What do you mean?" he asked, trying to buy himself more time.

He had been trying to think of ways around this conversation for hours now, and yet at zero hour, he still couldn't decide exactly how he wanted to handle things with his family. They deserved to know the truth about Sabrina, and they absolutely had to learn that they were under investigation. In fact, if he were under investigation, it was likely that other UCs were trying to break into their lives—other UCs who probably weren't as softhearted and kind as Sabrina.

And yet it would be immediately clear who the UC was in their lives as soon as he started talking. He wouldn't be able to hide her identity. At least Chad wouldn't want to kill her since she was an agent for the FBI...hopefully. Even though she didn't have a clue, they were all playing for the same team.

He would just have to figure a way out of this that worked for everyone and kept his family and Sabrina safe.

"You know exactly what I'm talking about, Trevor." Chad motioned toward the barn. "What happened up there on the mountain? Did you kill the family—is that why she's acting all weird around you? Or did you guys bump uglies?"

"Dude, seriously?" Trevor said, trying to look as innocent as possible. "Would I be this quiet if I'd taken the family out?"

"Good point," Chad said with a nod. "So then, you banged her?"

Trevor shook his head but was careful not to look

at his brother. His eyes would give it away. "Sabrina? She's a nice woman, but I have a feeling that she's not going to stick around here too much longer. Especially after what we found," he said, a bit proud of the way he'd maneuvered around lying to his brother. Some things were better left unsaid.

"Which was?"

"Somebody up there decided to spark a few rounds off at us. They were just warning shots, but somebody wanted us to get the message we weren't welcome."

He told him about the shooter and the campsite but left out his theory about who had been pulling the trigger and why. There was no use getting his brother up in arms about something he wasn't sure of just yet. All Chad needed to worry about was making sure that the affairs of the ranch were in order and that the Gray Wolves didn't find out where they were.

If nothing else, at least he could be fairly certain that it wasn't his family's enemies who were behind this and the Cussler guy's death.

"What, are you surprised that our squatters would have a problem with you chasing them down? Nobody likes being kicked out of their house," Chad said.

Now would've been the perfect time for Trevor to tell him the truth and explain all the problems they were facing, but he held back. "Chad, do you think we made a mistake coming back here?"

"What makes you ask that?" Chad asked with a worried expression on his face.

"Nothing," Trevor said with a shrug. "I've been thinking maybe the US isn't the best place for us. I know we thought we had amnesty here, but what if we don't? What if we peed in the wrong person's cornflakes, you know what I mean?"

"Clearly you're not telling me something," Chad said. "When you left here yesterday, you are all gung ho and ready to start making a new life here—even though it was boring. And now it's like you had a complete change of heart. You have to tell me why."

Trevor got up from the couch and strode over to the bay window that looked out toward the barn. The lights were on and the sliding door was open. Sabrina was unloading Zane. He watched as she backed him out of the trailer. "Call it a gut feeling or whatever you want, but I just think that maybe it's best if we bug out for a while—go somewhere in the Cayman Islands or something. Think about it, we could be lying on the white sand beach and drinking a cold one."

Chad stared at him like he was trying hard to figure him out. "Dude, Trevor, if you did something to upset Sabrina, we can figure it out—we don't need to get out of here. There a lot of housekeepers we could hire."

"Have you talked to Zoey at all while we were gone?" Trevor asked, trying to change the subject.

"Zoey said she's been watching all the channels, but so far she hasn't seen anything that would indicate the Gray Wolves have any idea where to find us." Chad got up and walked over and stood beside him at the window. "I know you're nervous, maybe that's what's going on with you, but I'm telling you this ranch is about the safest place we can possibly be. At least out here we have less of a chance of the Gray Wolves buying out some government agency in order to find us. I mean who is out here who would give two craps about us?"

Trevor's stomach dropped. What if Bayural had bought out someone at the FBI? Maybe they had sent Sabrina here to make sure they stayed while they got everything in place to take them out. But then, if that were the case, wouldn't they have just taken out a contract with a merc?

"Let's get the hell out of here," Trevor said, turning his back to the window.

"What? And what about Sabrina?" Chad asked, not stopping to ask him what he was thinking. His brother knew him well enough that if he said it was time to go, it was time to go. He could explain it to him later.

"We'll take her with us—if she wants to go."

"I knew you banged her," Chad said with a satisfied laugh as they rushed down the hall to their bedrooms to grab their bug-out bags.

Trevor was pulling out the .50cal from behind his mattress when the front door of the house slammed open.

"Trevor!" Sabrina yelled, her voice frantic.

The Gray Wolves were coming for them; he could feel it even though everything hadn't yet quite clicked into place. "What?" He dropped his bag and his gun case and sprinted out of the room, pulling his SIG Sauer from his holster and readying himself for whatever—or whoever—he was about to meet at that door.

Sabrina was standing at the front door, her hands over her mouth.

He lowered his weapon when he saw no one was behind her. "Are you okay? What's going on?" he asked, the words rushing out like it was a single syllable.

"There…" She motioned behind her. "There's a man out there, inside the last barn stall. He…he's been shot."

"Is he still alive?" Trevor hurried to her as Chad came running down the hall and to the living room.

She shrugged. "There was blood everywhere. I didn't stay to check him out."

"How long have you been home, Chad?" Trevor asked.

"I got back last night at midnight. Haven't left since then."

"And you didn't hear anyone coming or going, any cars?" Trevor asked.

Chad shook his head. "It's been quiet. No one."

"Stay in the house," Trevor said. "Make sure you watch our six. Whoever shot the guy is probably still out there—and they are probably gunning for us as well."

As he ran toward the barn he couldn't help but wonder if he was wrong and their shooter was already long gone—he had to hope, but he wasn't going to risk it.

If Bayural or his men were here, they could have easily taken Chad out while he'd been sitting watching television in the living room. From the right vantage point, Chad would never have known that anyone was ever even out there.

Whoever was behind these killings was doing their best to frighten them into submission. He couldn't let the killer get away with their murderous rampage any longer.

"Did you recognize the guy?" he asked Sabrina as he followed her into the barn.

Sabrina shook her head as she pointed toward the last stall. "He's in there."

Zane was nickering, his sound high-pitched and scared as he trotted nervously around the stall. Just like Trevor, he must have been able to feel the danger in the air.

Trevor walked to the last stall, half-afraid of what

he would find. The blood was splattered over the wood paneling and there was a bloody handprint smeared down the far wall. "Hello?" he called, hoping that the man would answer. But there was little chance that the man was alive on the other side of the gate.

There was no answer.

He unclicked the latch and opened the gate, stepping into the stall. There, against the wall closest to him and tucked back into the corner of the room, was the man. He had scraggly gray locks and hair was sprouting from his ears. On his neck was a long, puckered scar as though someone had once tried to cut his throat but failed.

His hands were covered in blood and palms up in his lap, and his head was leaning haphazardly to the side. There was something about the man's face that looked familiar. He'd seen those same eyes and that shape face before—in fact, he looked almost identical, albeit slightly older, to the man in the shack. Trevor had to be looking at another of the Cussler brothers.

He walked over to the man and placed his fingers against his neck, hoping against all hope that there would be some faint pulse, but he found nothing but a sickening chill. He pulled his hand back. Algor mortis had started to set in.

Trevor moved to the man's feet and pulled back the leg of his pants, careful not to touch too much and leave behind any trace evidence. The guy had been sitting with his knees up and, even though Trevor pulled at his jeans, his legs stayed bent due to the effects of rigor. He'd definitely been down at least a few hours. Around twelve and he would have been completely immobile, but there was still a bit of pliability in his limbs.

Who in the hell was killing this family? And had they planned to murder the man here or had the man come here to die after he had been shot—making it look like Trevor and his family were responsible for his death?

"Is he alive?" Sabrina asked, but there was a resignation in her voice that told him she already knew the answer.

He didn't respond. Sabrina stopped behind the opened gate and looked inside; her gaze moved to the dead man. Maybe the poor light in the barn was causing him to see things, but he could have sworn that her face had grown a shade paler.

"You don't have to be in here," he said, moving closer to her and taking her hand. "You don't have to pretend to be tougher than you are with me."

She opened her mouth to speak as she looked up at him. There was a renewed softness in her eyes, and the look reminded him of when they had been making love and her body had begged him for her release.

"It's okay," he said, giving her a soft kiss to her forehead. "I've got this."

She took a step back so the man's dead body was out of her view, but she didn't leave. "What are we going to do, Trevor?"

He hadn't gotten that far yet.

This really should have been a case for the local cops, but calling them in would lead to a whole slew of questions he wasn't ready or willing to answer. It would only land them in deeper trouble. Yet they couldn't just wait for this body to disappear like they had the last, not with so many possible variables.

His first thought was for her to call her people at the FBI, but if they were in any way connected to this case, they wouldn't be coming in as allies. They weren't an option.

He'd have to call in a few of his friends at the CIA. They didn't typically work within the borders of the States, but undoubtedly his people knew some folks who could help him sweep this man's death under the rug.

Though sweeping it under the rug last time had certainly done them no favors. They needed to find answers and fast.

"You don't think your brother has a hand in this, do you?" Sabrina asked, her voice soft and smooth as though she was trying to be careful and not sound too accusatory.

He appreciated her effort, but her question still ruffled his feathers. "Chad wouldn't be stupid enough to kill a guy and leave his body sitting out here."

"Unless he wanted to set us up. He doesn't have a reason to want to drive you off the ranch, does he?" Sabrina asked.

He tried to control the anger that rolled through him. "No. He didn't do this. He wouldn't do this. My family are the only people I can really trust."

She visibly cringed at his unintentional jab.

"I just mean that he wouldn't have let us walk out here and work in the barn if he'd left this guy to cool down before getting rid of his remains."

"But you admit your brother is fully capable of pulling the trigger?"

"Look, Sabrina," he said, running his hands over the stubble that had grown on his cheeks over the last few days. "Anyone is capable of killing under the right circumstances. My brother is perhaps more likely to find himself in those kinds of circumstances than most, but that doesn't mean he is an evil man. He doesn't just go around killing people."

"I'm sorry, I know you're right," Sabrina said, leaning against the doorjamb. "I'm just…tired."

"I know you want to find an answer to this that doesn't point back to your people at the FBI, but you need to stop looking in my direction in order to figure out who is behind these killings—at least in the direction of my family. I'm telling you, we aren't the ones keeping secrets from one another."

She nodded. "I'd be lying if I said I wasn't a little jealous. Your family…it's one of a kind. I would like to have a group of people who I could always depend on."

His anger dissipated. He knew what it felt like to be lost, so he could empathize with what she was going through right now. In fact, he had to wonder if he was the only one she could really trust.

It seemed crazy how far they had come since they first met each other. He would never have guessed that this was how they would've played out. Aside from the dead guys, he wasn't sure he would change anything. He liked the fact that she was nearly as dangerous as him.

"Did you figure out where he was shot?" she asked, clearly trying to change the subject.

That was something else he appreciated about her—she was just as avoidant of feelings as he was. Sure, it may not have been the healthiest response, but it certainly kept one from getting hurt.

He stepped closer to the man. There was a small hole in his jacket just over his heart. Flipping back the edge of the coat, there was a small wound in his chest. Blood had seeped out and run down from the wound and had pooled at the top of his large belly before slipping down onto his jeans. "Looks like it was a single shot. Likely at least ten feet away."

There was the crunch of tires on the gravel of the parking lot just outside the barn. Trevor flipped the man's jacket closed, and as he did so he noticed the smear of blood on his own hands.

As he turned away, he saw a small hole in the wall. Lodged in the soft wood was a bullet.

Sabrina looked at him. "You think we should go out there?"

There was the sound of footsteps in the gravel as somebody made their way toward them.

Trevor rushed out of the stall, wiping his hands on the backside of his jeans. As he turned to face the door, a man came into view. Not just a man, but a deputy sheriff. He was all brassed up, complete with a Kevlar vest underneath his uniform. He looked to be in his midthirties, maybe. His hair was shorn and starting to recede just above the temples, and his forehead was littered with the wrinkles of someone who worried often.

He forced a smile as he walked toward the man. Zane's whinnies intensified from inside the horse's stall.

"Hey, Deputy, how's it going?" Trevor said, trying to sound amicable.

The deputy gave him a two-fingered wave. "Good," he said, sounding as tight and rigid as the vest he was wearing. "Anything going on out here that I need to know about?"

Sabrina gave him a confused look. "Nothing I can think of, Deputy."

The man chuckled. "May I ask your name, please?" The question was more of an order than a nicety.

Trevor strode toward him, moving with as much confidence as he possibly could. He extended his hand. "The name's Trevor Martin, you?"

The man gave him a strong shake of the hand, so strong it came across as an act of dominance—as though he wanted Trevor to know that he was at the head of the hierarchy here. "The name's Wyatt." A smile broke across the man's face. "Did Gwen tell you I was coming?"

Sabrina stepped between them as she shook her head. "Trevor, this is Wyatt, Gwen's husband."

"Oh," Trevor said, a wave of relief crashing over him. "Nice to meet you, man. Gwen's a fantastic woman. I'm proud to have her as a cousin."

"She is that." Wyatt glanced around the barn. "It's been a long time since I've been in here. I helped Gwen and her mom get this place together so you guys could move in. Hope you found everything in order."

Trevor nodded, but his mind went straight to the dead man in the last stall. "Everything's been great, but we are still getting organized on our end. I'm thinking my sister and other brother should be descending upon the ranch in the next few weeks."

Wyatt nodded. "That'll be great. It'll be nice to have some more family close. I know Gwen's been awful lonely since her sister passed away. She's been looking forward to getting to know you guys a little better."

Trevor nodded. "I was so sorry to hear about Bianca's death. At least they caught the person responsible."

"Yeah, best part of my job is getting to watch the guilty pay for their crimes."

Panic rose within him.

Zane nickered as he stuck his head out of his stall door and looked toward them.

"Ah," Wyatt said, looking toward the horse, "my old boy's here." He walked by them to the horse and gave the gelding a good scratch under the mane. The horse seemed to soften under Wyatt's touch.

"This your horse?" Sabrina asked as she stepped around Wyatt like she was trying to keep him from walking farther into the barn.

"Yep," Wyatt said. "He and I have been buddies for a long time. Gwen told me you had taken them up riding, but I figured you had brought them back to Dunrovin by now."

"Actually, we just got back from our ride. We were gonna take a rest, and then bring them back to you guys in the morning." Trevor motioned outside. "In fact, we haven't even unloaded the other horse yet. If you wanted, since you're here, we could load up Zane and—"

"No worries. Gwen and I both know how it is." Wyatt waved him quiet. "Did you guys just run the fences or did you go up the mountain a bit?"

Trevor wasn't sure if Wyatt was testing him or

not, but he didn't want to give him the wrong answer. "Yeah, we ran up to the top of Rye Creek. Nice area up there."

"When you get up there in those high mountains the last thing you want to do is come back to real life." Wyatt looked to Sabrina and then back to Trevor and gave him a knowing wink. "And you can keep the horses here as long as you like. Zane isn't our main guest horse, so he's not in high demand. It does him some good to get in some trail time."

Why did everyone assume that something had happened between him and Sabrina out there in the woods? Not that they were wrong. It just hardly seemed like it was anyone else's business.

"Zane is such a good boy," Sabrina said, bridging the gap for him. "It was a nice ride."

"Did you run into the squatters?" Wyatt pressed.

Did the man know something he didn't? Or was he looking for him to supply him with some kind of information? Regardless, his questions were making him unsettled.

"Nope, but we saw a camp they may have been using as a base."

Wyatt nodded. "Good thing. That family can be a wild bunch. And they like to take potshots at people they don't know or don't like."

"Good to know."

Sabrina smiled, the effect dazzling. "Was there something we could help you with, Wyatt?"

He turned and looked toward the end of the barn like he was some kind of damned bloodhound. "Actually, I was here because we got an anonymous tip."

"What?" Trevor asked, his voice taking on an unwanted higher pitch.

"Someone said they heard some shooting coming from out here. They said it sounded like it was coming from inside one of the buildings." Wyatt turned to them. "You guys know anything about that?"

There wasn't anyone within earshot of this place, and certainly shooting at a ranch wouldn't have rung any warning bells. Someone had called in the tip on purpose—they probably wanted Wyatt to stumble onto the body.

They'd been set up.

"Don't know anything about that. Like we said, we just got back from our ride," Trevor said.

Wyatt looked to Sabrina and she nodded in support. "Anyone around here while you were gone?"

If Wyatt looked outside and toward the house he would have likely seen Chad standing near the front window. They couldn't lie and cover his brother's whereabouts—but as far as Wyatt was concerned, he seemed to be out here for nothing more than some suspicious activity. There was no use in lying.

"Actually, my brother Chad was here. He didn't tell me he'd heard anything. And I'm pretty sure he's been watching old football games all day."

Wyatt laughed. "Dang, I want your brother's life. That is just so long as he was drinking beer and eating Doritos as well."

"You know it," Trevor said, giving his cousin's husband a jovial slap on the back. He started to move toward the barn door in an effort to get the man out of the death zone. "You want to come inside and ask him about it?"

"Sure thing. It'd be nice to meet the rest of the family." Wyatt walked toward the front of the barn.

Trevor was careful to stay behind the man so he couldn't see the blood that was likely smeared on the seat of his pants. That would be hard to explain away.

They walked back to the house and Chad met them with an open door. "Hey, bro, this is Wyatt Fitzgerald, Gwen's husband."

Chad wiped his cheese-dusted fingers on the legs of his sweatpants and gave Wyatt a quick shake. "Nice to meet you, man. What can we do for you?" Chad gave Trevor a worried look, and Trevor shook his head in an attempt to convey the fact the deputy knew nothing about the body.

"We have a report of some shooting going on out here. You know anything about it?" Wyatt asked.

Chad nodded for a moment, and Trevor could see the wheels turning in his brother's head. "Hey, yeah… Sorry, that was me. I saw a coyote out there. Wanted to scare 'im off."

Wyatt nodded. "It work?"

Chad laughed. "Not gonna lie, been a lot of beers in the belly today—that, or the aim was a bit off on the old .22."

"I hear you, coz," Wyatt said as he started to warm to them. "If I was retired I would probably be doing just about the same thing—though Gwen may have something to say about that."

Chad laughed. "There are some benefits to being a single guy."

Sabrina's brow lifted as she gave him a look of disdain. "If you keep up the sweatpants and Doritos fingers, the last thing you have to worry about is some poor woman falling in love with you."

"Oh, burn." Wyatt laughed. "It's funny how women have a way of making us step up our game, isn't it?" He looked to Trevor.

The game—that was one word to describe exactly what was going on in their lives. And this game of murder was one game he couldn't lose.

Chapter Twelve

What in the name of all that was holy was going on around here? Sabrina wished the answers would suddenly appear and everything would make sense.

As the guys continued to talk, her mind wandered. It seemed possible that the Cusslers and the other hillbilly family could have been in some kind of backwoods war, and this was their way of telling the Martins they weren't welcome at the ranch. Maybe it was the second family, and they were figuring they could kill two birds with one stone—the Cussler man, and the Martins' chance of having a peaceful life out here.

But they couldn't have known the Martins wouldn't call the police—unless they been watching them dance around the issue of the dead body in the shack. They must have been watching, and had pieced it together that the thing Trevor and his family feared most was drawing attention from the cops. And they had set the boys up to take this fall.

The thought of being under surveillance made the hairs on the back of her neck stand on end. And yet it made her feel like a hypocrite as she had been doing almost exactly the same thing to Trevor and the Martins for the last little while.

Wyatt gave her an acknowledging nod goodbye as he made his way out the door and toward his patrol unit. "If you guys need anything, or want to meet up for supper sometime, give us a call. Gwen's looking forward to getting together." Wyatt opened the door to his car and the small Chihuahua from Dunrovin jumped out and scurried off in the direction of the barn.

"Francesca," he called after the dog, and as he called the animal's name a look of embarrassment crossed over his face. "I swear I didn't name the dog," he called as he chased after the little thing.

Sabrina ran after them in hopes of catching the dog before she could make her way too far into the barn. The opportunity to tell Wyatt about the body had already come and gone, and if he found the man's body they'd all be arrested for obstruction of justice and possibly tampering with evidence.

She'd have to expose who she was and why she was here to Chad and Wyatt, and what little chance remained of her finishing this investigation and clearing the family's name would go up in dust.

"Here, pup!" Trevor called, his voice frantic.

Wyatt rushed ahead of them into the barn and disappeared.

She hurried to the door, but it was too late. The deputy stood beside the small dog, who was sniffing manically at the base of the last stall. Francesca barked, panting as she looked up to her master. The little dog looked proud of her investigative skills. It almost would have been cute if it hadn't have just blown her cover.

Trevor slipped his hand into hers and gave it a squeeze. For a second, she considered running and getting out of there, but she wasn't the kind who was going to run from her problems. She had to face whatever was coming thanks to that little dog.

She never really considered herself a full-blown cat person until now.

Wyatt stood there in silence, simply staring into the stall for a long moment before turning to them, a dark expression on his features. "How long did you guys say you been back from your ride?"

Trevor took the lead. He shrugged. "Not long. Like we said, we just unloaded Zane. Why, what's up?"

Smart. Feigning ignorance was the only plausible excuse for what the deputy had just found.

Wyatt turned back toward the stall. "I hate to tell you guys this but it looks like I'm gonna need to call out a few more friends of mine."

"Why?" Sabrina asked, she and Trevor took a few steps toward him.

Wyatt held up his hand. "Stop right there. I can't have you coming any closer. Not until I can get my team out here to investigate."

Trevor was already close enough to see the body from the open gate. He motioned for Sabrina to back up. "You don't need to see this." She wasn't sure whether Wyatt wanted to keep them away from the body to see exactly how much they knew, or if he just wanted to protect them from seeing something traumatic.

"Trevor, run inside and get Chad. He needs to know what's going on out here," she said, and leaning in close she whispered, "Don't forget to change your pants. Put them somewhere safe." She gave him a peck on the cheek in hopes it wouldn't look like she had been whispering directions.

Trevor looked unflappable, and his stoicism made her chest tighten with something much too close to love. She had to respect a man who held a great poker face even under the most strenuous of circumstances.

"I'll be right back," Trevor said, but Wyatt was focused on the body.

As Trevor rushed from the barn, she walked toward Wyatt, ignoring his request for her to stay back. She had to pretend to look at the body for the first time.

She stopped beside Wyatt as the man's body came

into view. She clapped her hands over her mouth in an attempt to look as surprised as she had been a little while ago. "Do you know who this man is?"

Wyatt turned to her. "I told you not to come back here. You need to leave the barn, right now. Don't touch anything."

Reality came rushing in and Sabrina realized what she had to do. "Wyatt, we knew about the body. We had just found him before you arrived." Before Wyatt ran away with this, she had to tell him the truth…no matter how badly she didn't want to. "I'm a special agent with the FBI, currently I'm investigating a series of crimes. I'm close to cracking the case, but if you pull your men out here, I'm afraid that my cover and my investigation will be blown."

"That can't be true," Wyatt said, staring at her in disbelief.

"Call your sheriff. My people have been in contact with him throughout the investigation. He's the one we briefed when we came in, so he knew what was going on. I wasn't planning on being here too much longer. The Bureau is breathing down my neck. They want results."

"And are you going to get them?" Wyatt asked. "Did you get everything you needed?"

"I'm starting to figure things out. But with this guy's death, I'm afraid there's more going on here than I had anticipated. I need to talk to my handler about what's happened. However, I doubt I will get an extension on my assignment."

"How much longer do you have?"

"Less than a week," Sabrina said. She scuffed her boot around in the spent hay on the barn's floor, kicking up the scent of dirt and horse manure. "It's my hope that I can clear the Martins' name and head off to my next assignment."

Wyatt nodded, but he didn't say anything. The barn door squeaked as Trevor and Chad pushed it open a bit wider and walked in. Chad had the look of a deer in the headlights as he stared at Wyatt.

Wyatt cleared his throat and turned toward the brothers. "Did your brother tell you what we found?"

Chad nodded.

"I'm going to have my crew come in and investigate this man's death. It would make it a whole lot easier if you tell me what actually happened here before my team lays this on you." Wyatt stepped over to the pile of hay bales and leaned against them, crossing his arms over his chest. "You're my family by marriage and I'm going to do everything in my power to make sure you guys stay out of harm's way, but you have to tell me the truth." He looked directly at Sabrina and gave her an almost-imperceptible wink.

It did little to quell the nerves that were building within her. From what she'd heard about the Mystery, Montana, sheriff's department, their forensics team left much to be desired. Hopefully, that would work to her advantage.

But she still couldn't have anyone blowing her cover.

"Let's try this again," Wyatt said to Chad. "Was this man the coyote you were shooting at today?"

Chad rubbed his hands over his face. "I only found out about this dead guy about four seconds before I walked out here. If I had shot him, I would tell you it was in self-defense or something. But I haven't even seen the guy yet." He waved toward the end of the barn.

"The man's name is Earl Cussler. He's the second oldest of the Cussler boys. They are all as mean as rattlesnakes, so if you had admitted to shooting him in self-defense, I would've believed it. However, as it stands, this isn't going to work for me or my department." Wyatt took out his cell phone and glanced down at the buzzing device. "I want you to all go inside before I call in my team."

She turned to leave the barn, but Wyatt motioned her back. "Trevor, I'll be along in a second."

Trevor frowned at her as he made his way out of the barn. "Are you sure?" he whispered, glancing at his cousin's husband.

She nodded. "It's going to be fine."

She watched as Trevor and Chad went back to the main house. They were chatting as they walked, but she couldn't hear exactly what they were saying. No doubt it was something about how much trouble they were going to be in once everything broke. She was afraid she wouldn't be able to help them.

"Who's your handler?" he asked, pulling her attention back to him.

"His name's Mike Couer," she said, a bitter taste filling her mouth. "If you talk to him, take what he says about me with a grain of salt. He and I used to be a thing."

Wyatt chuckled, the sound out of place and haunting in the impromptu crypt. "I thought the Bureau looked down on that."

"They do, but it didn't last long—only long enough to make us realize it was a mistake."

"And to dislike each other?" Wyatt asked.

She couldn't deny it. "Let's just say, if you call him about me, I can't guarantee exactly what he's going to say. I was hoping to use this case to get out of the trenches and into another field office."

Hopefully Wyatt wouldn't judge her unfairly for the mistakes she had made. He was the only shot they had at keeping things under wraps for a bit.

"If that's all true," Wyatt said, leaning back on the hay, "then I understand why you're in a rush to end this investigation. There's nothing more fun than having to deal with your ex's crazy behavior all the time. My family knows exactly how far an ex will go to wreak havoc on a person's life."

"Yeah, Gwen told me what you guys had gone

through." She hoped this commonality would act as a bridge between them, a bridge that would lead to her getting her way. "I'm sorry to hear about the mayhem. Sounds like a lot of people died." She hadn't meant to sound so crass and un-empathetic, but her tone came out all wrong.

Wyatt looked at her with surprise, as though he had heard the hardness in her words as well. "You weren't investigating my family, were you?"

She didn't want to lie to him. "Your family drew a bit of scrutiny thanks to your recent run-in with the law, but you were all cleared. However, your name was scattered throughout my files. Just like the Martins, upon coming here and digging a bit, it was easy to see that you weren't criminals—just at the wrong end of someone's sights."

"That's an understatement. It was one hell of a Christmas."

"I can only imagine how you guys must've been feeling."

"Yeah, but even with all the upheaval, a lot of good came from my family's legal troubles."

It was no secret that everything had worked in his family's favor financially, and they had added several family members to their tree. Again, she was witness to a family that seemed to figure out how to stay together, no matter what. She'd never know what that would be like.

"Then I'm sure you can understand—maybe better than anyone—what I want to happen for the Martins." She brushed her hair out of her face. "I know what I'm about to ask isn't aboveboard, but I want you to consider it just for a couple seconds before you give me your answer. Deal?"

The darkness returned to his features, but he nodded.

"All I'm asking," she continued, "is that you give me twenty-four hours. Tomorrow at this time, regardless of if I have this figured out or not, I will call you and report this guy's death and your crew can come and get the body. You and your team will have access to everything I can give you, and I'll talk to Chad and make sure he had nothing to do with this. However, for the time being, I need you to turn a blind eye. Call this a favor for the FBI, a favor I will happily return if the need arises."

"I knew that's where you were going." Wyatt stood up and readjusted his Kevlar vest. "If I don't hear from you in exactly twenty-four hours, I will be standing on that doorstep. I will come after you, and your ex won't be your only enemy in law enforcement. Got it?"

"You can trust me, Wyatt. Thank you for this. I know it's hard to do something like this, but know you're doing the right thing."

"I hope so. I hope you realize you're not just putting your own ass on the line, but mine as well. I don't need this kind of trouble, but I've learned having friends in high places can make all the difference. Don't you be forgetting you owe me."

She had expected some of the weight to be lifted off her shoulders, but as Wyatt walked out of the barn, it was like the entire world was upon her. They'd have to get to the bottom of this fast, or her entire world—and everyone else's around her—would come crashing down.

Chapter Thirteen

Trevor hated that he'd had to leave Sabrina in the barn alone with Wyatt. He could only guess what they'd talked about, but no doubt she'd had to let him in on her secret.

Wyatt walked out of the barn and got into the squad car. Starting it up, he drove away. *Holy crap*, what had she said to him? The deputy hadn't seemed like the type who would walk away from a case like this. Family or not, he hadn't expected any sort of favors from the man.

"Dude, did you see that?" Chad asked, pointing out the window.

"I'll be right back," he said, already half out the door.

Sabrina met him halfway; her hands were up like she was surrendering to him. "It's going to be okay, Trevor. I made a deal with him."

"Is he dropping his investigation?" he asked, taking hold of her shoulders and looking her in the eye.

Her whole body tensed underneath his touch. "Far from it. We have twenty-four hours. That's it. Then all hell's going to break loose. And I would guess that at least Chad will be arrested. And you wouldn't be far behind…nor would I."

"Are you kidding me? We barely have a clue about what's going on out here. And yet you think we can solve this in a day?" She must've lost her mind. He was going to jail. They had to run. And yet if they did, it would make them look incredibly guilty. And she would have to answer for their leaving.

"Trevor, there's something I didn't tell you before. I didn't think it was important, but now with this…" She nibbled at her lip. "My handler at the Missoula resident agency, his name is Mike. He's my ex."

As she said the man's name, it looked as though she was in pain. She must hate the man. He could only imagine the kind of drama that would unfold inside the close quarters that was the FBI. It was known for being fraught with varying levels of corruption and mistrust—none more so than the last few years. Lately, it was as if everything had gone crazy in the Bureau. It was a wonder that she even had a job if she'd made the mistake of falling for her boss. In fact, this Mike guy was lucky that she hadn't gone after him for any sort of predatory behavior. The man had to be one hell of a winner if he was preying on women within his agency in order to get some.

On the other hand, perhaps she really had loved the guy and it was a relationship built upon real feelings. It was easy enough to see how something like that could come about, with forced proximity and all, but he would have thought a man in an authority position would have made the choice to not put them both in jeopardy. Then again, Sabrina was of her own mind. She had made choices—this wasn't sitting on just the shoulders of her boss. She had to have understood what kind of position she was putting herself in.

He needed to distance himself from her. Not that he didn't already know that. He just couldn't get over how sweet her lips had tasted, and how it felt when her body was pressed against him. In a weird way, his heart had felt as shriveled and emaciated as a starving man, but when she'd entered his life it was like it had started to beat again and grow stronger thanks to the nourishment that came with her presence.

Ugh, he was being so ridiculous.

"Do you still love him?" he asked without thinking.

From the look on her face, the question had clearly come out of left field. "No."

Her curtness didn't help him feel any better.

He counted his breaths until he reached ten and his heart rate lowered. He had to keep his wits about him. "Okay, so do you think this guy is gunning for you…for us?"

She chewed on her lip until a tiny bit of blood dotted its pink curve. "I want to say no, but the truth is I'm not sure. He's been pushing me hard throughout this investigation. He rushed it through the bureaucracy. What normally takes six months to get approvals for, he did in a matter of weeks. I don't know how he did it, but it may be part of the reason he needs us to get to the bottom of this so quickly."

"*This*—as in my family?" Even he could hear the hurt in his voice.

"I meant my investigation." She gave him an apologetic smile. "Mike is probably on the warpath. He likely overextended himself and promised results that, frankly, I'm not sure I'm going to be able deliver on."

"Do you think if you went to the offices that you could get a better feel for what's going on with Mike?" Part of him wanted to go with her, to ensure she was safe. Yet the last place he needed to be seen was sitting outside a federal building. Even with his connections with the CIA, those watching wouldn't appreciate his suspicious behavior.

"Mike is not the kind of guy you can get an easy read on. The FBI has trained that out of him. He's like talking to a wall."

With that kind of description, he wasn't sure how she had ever found herself falling for such a guy.

Though if he looked at himself closely, he was probably cut from the same cloth as Mike. Again, he found himself lacking. He had to hope he was nothing like a possibly crooked agent. Though Sabrina hadn't always thought him capable, he was a man guided by morals. Which only made all of this more difficult.

"I think we should go, but I'll need stay out of sight. The last thing we need is you showing up to the regional headquarters with the man you are in charge of investigating." Trevor pulled the keys from his pocket.

Sabrina sniggered. "I can't even imagine how badly that would play out."

"Well, you don't have to as long as things go smoothly. In and out, okay?" he said with a raise of the brow.

"All right, but no matter what happens you have to stay out of the limelight."

He nodded. "I'll unhitch the trailer if you unload the other horse."

They made quick work of it. Sabrina wiped her hands on the leg of her pants as she closed up the barn and turned to him. "What about Chad and the cops? You don't think he'll blow my cover, do you?"

"Chad is a knot head, but he's not stupid. You're safe when it comes to my family and them keeping their mouths shut." He lifted the keys. "You want to drive?" he teased.

"If we want to get there in one piece, I better."

He threw the keys to her with a chuckle.

It wasn't too long a drive to Missoula. With each passing mile, more nerves started to fill him. It felt almost as if he was back in Adana, and the gun trade was just about to go down with Trish. This same sense of foreboding had filled him then. If something happened to Sabrina, like it had to Trish, he wasn't sure he could keep on living. The crushing blow of losing his sister had been all the tragedy he could bear. He couldn't lose someone else he loved.

"When I get out, I want you to take the wheel and drive over to the Staggering Ox. Order a sandwich, and I'll get an Uber and catch up."

He didn't like the plan, but he was in no position to argue. If something happened inside the federal building, he'd never get access in time to save her. But Mike didn't sound like a guy who would get caught making a visible threat against another agent.

Regardless of how uncomfortable it made him, he had to trust her judgment. She was going to do what she had to do for them and for their investigation. Though he had never intended on them working together, in this moment, he realized that was exactly what they were doing—inadvertently, their relationship had morphed into something new…something that *fit*.

No. He was just seeing things that weren't really possible. Sure, they could work this thing together, but that didn't mean anything for the future. This was nothing more than an isolated incident including some extenuating circumstances—circumstances that, for this moment in time, had them working toward the same goal. Once they got to the bottom of this and found their murderer they would be forced to go their separate ways.

She pulled the truck to a stop about a block away from the Fed office and got out.

"Be careful," he said, ignoring the apprehension that was gnawing away in his gut. "If you need me, I can be back within a couple of minutes."

She nodded. Her features were tight, as though she were feeling some of the same nervous energy that he was—it did nothing to make him feel better. He wanted to tell her to stop, that they could do something else, something less risky, something that wouldn't put her square at the center of Mike's radar. And yet, the leads—which all pointed at corruption—had brought them here.

This was the only way...anything else would take them far longer than the time they had been allowed.

In the meantime, he had some work of his own to do.

He watched for a moment as she walked down the sidewalk. She was still wearing her dirty clothes from the trail ride, and there was mud on her boots. She looked like anything but a special agent.

He put the truck in gear and looked up the sandwich shop on his phone, then made his way across town. The hole-in-the-wall restaurant comprised about a dozen tables, all of which were covered in inlaid comic book pages. It carried a certain charm. And as he walked toward the register, the scent of warm bread and fresh lettuce filled the air. It made his mouth water as he realized that the last time he had eaten was when they were up on the mountain. His stomach grumbled and twisted in his belly.

He ordered a couple of sandwiches and went outside to make a phone call while he waited for them to be ready.

He pulled out his phone and dialed his point person within the CIA.

She answered on the first ring. "Trevor, what's going on, man?" She sounded excited in her normal, brusque way.

"Hey. I'm working a case and I need your help."

"I thought you had taken a leave of absence," she said with a chuckle.

"You know full well that even when we're not working, we're working."

"I wouldn't know. I'm never blessed with free time, you lucky bastard," she teased.

He'd always appreciated Tina's ability to not delve down the dark and disturbing rabbit hole that was the past—she knew exactly why he had taken time away from the CIA, and why he was likely going to choose to retire, and yet she avoided bringing up his sister.

"I'm what we're calling lucky now?" He laughed.

"I'd hate to see what it means to be one of the un-lucky ones."

Tina laughed. "What do you want? I know you didn't call me just to be an ornery ass."

"I've been dealing with some DOAs."

"Because of course you have," Tina said, inter-rupting.

"Ha ha, you know if your job ever craps out at the agency, you can always become a comedian."

"I'm not half as funny as your face is looking."

"Anyone ever tell you you're a real pain in the butt?"

"Every day."

"Actually, I was calling about a friend of mine in the Bureau. We have reason to believe that there's some interoffice corruption going on."

There was a long silence on the other end of the line.

"Dude, Trevor, if you're right, you don't want to get within a thousand miles of that kind of thing. Pol-itics has a way of ruining even the best reputations."

Tina was right, but in this instance, he didn't have a whole lot of choice in the matter—he was already deeply involved. "I hear you. I do. However, that ship has sailed. What I need from you is for you to help me run some ballistic tests. I have reason to be-lieve that the rounds may belong to a federally issued weapon. I just need to know for sure. That something you can help me with?"

"Are you serious? Are you really asking me to stick my neck out and take part in defaming an FBI agent? You'd be putting my job at risk, you realize that, right?" Tina asked, but from her tone he couldn't decide whether or not she was being serious or kidding around. Either way he wouldn't have been surprised.

"Is that a no?"

Tina chuckled. "Pfft, come on now, you know we're supposed to be all buddy-buddy with our FBI brethren, but nothing would make me happier than knocking the hierarchy down a peg or two. Get them to the Montana State Crime Lab. I have some friends there who owe me a favor."

"I knew I could count on you," Trevor said. "I'll get the samples there as soon as I can. They should be to you within the hour. And hey, thanks."

"I've always got your back. And next time we work together, I'll make sure you get the first crappy detail that comes along."

"I'd expect nothing less."

She hung up. He sent a quick text to Chad, asking him to run out to the barn and pull the round that was embedded in the wood of the stall.

The waiter walked out of the sandwich shop, carrying a paper bag of sandwiches. "Thanks," Trevor said, handing him a ten-dollar tip.

He walked back to the truck and sat down with his sandwich. He'd forgotten to order drinks, son of a gun. He slipped his sandwich back into the bag and was just about to get out as his phone rang. It was Sabrina. Just the sight of her name made the bite of sandwich he'd eaten sit poorly in his stomach. Hopefully she was okay.

"Do you need help?" he asked, bypassing any pleasantries.

"Mike isn't here. No one has seen him in the office in a couple of days. But they were acting strange, like they were hiding something." She sounded worried.

"And no one knows where he's at?" Trevor put his phone on speaker, sat back in his seat and slammed the truck door closed. He revved the engine and screamed out of the parking lot, hurrying back to get to her.

At least he didn't have to worry about Mike taking potshots at her, and she wasn't in immediate danger, but that didn't mean they were out of the woods yet.

"It doesn't sound like he's been seen or heard from in days. People are concerned and looking into his disappearance. This kind of behavior is very unlike him."

Something was going on in her office. Something that surely wouldn't play out in her favor.

"You didn't talk to anyone about our investigation into your team at the FBI, did you?"

"No, never. I couldn't."

Trevor ran through a yellow light as it turned red. Right now, he didn't care about following rules. He just had to get to Sabrina and make sure she was safe.

"You're not driving like a bat out of hell, are you?" Sabrina asked, but there was a hard edge to her voice as she teased him.

"I have no idea what you're talking about." He glanced at the road signs. "I'll be out front to pick you up in a minute. Be outside."

She laughed, but he could hear the echo of a stairwell and her footfalls as she must have been running down stairs. "It's okay, Trevor. I'm fine. You know you don't need to worry about me."

"I'm not," he lied. "I'm approaching one block due east of the front entrance."

The front door of the building opened and Sabrina walked outside. There was a muffled cry as she dropped her phone and it clattered onto the sidewalk. The line went dead. A group of agents surrounded her. She put her hands up and said something. She glanced in his direction, terror in her eyes. Her mouth opened, and from the distance it looked as though she was telling him to stay back.

He pulled the truck over just as the agent closest to Trevor took Sabrina down to the ground.

What in the hell is going on?

He couldn't just rush in there and fix things. If he did, it would likely only end up with him getting arrested and Sabrina getting fired for misconduct. But that didn't stop him.

He got out of the truck, only half-aware of the traffic that was passing around him. He ran down the street. "I demand you tell me what's going on here."

An older man, probably in his midfifties, sent him a dangerous smile. "I know exactly who you are, Trevor, and if you think your connections give you any right to know what is going on here, you are sorely mistaken." The man had to be Mike, Sabrina's ex. He seemed like exactly the jerk that she had described—with his salt-and-pepper hair, his silver fox looks and his arrogant swagger.

"What do you know, jackass?" Trevor sneered.

"Oh, I heard all about how you got fired from Spookville for your role in getting your sister killed." Mike stepped away and waved back the agents around him. "Sounds like you have your hands in all kinds of pots. I just wish it could have been us that found the information that proved it. As it was, Agent Parker here… Well, she lost her edge."

He didn't know what the hell he was talking about. Just like everything else about this investigation, it appeared as though he only had half the information—the half that made him want to punch Mike in the face.

"Sabrina," he said, pushing the arresting officer back and helping her up. "Are you okay?"

"Trevor, it is far from your best interest to get involved. I have it on good authority that you're just a few days away from this happening to you as well." Mike put his hand on the gun at his side, threatening him. "Actually, I bet I'd get a slap on the back for bringing you in for your role in the murders of Earl and Owen Cussler. Former CIA or not, murder is murder."

There were a lot of things that Trevor was guilty of, but not that. "And what genius came up with this theory?" He looked directly at Mike. "I'm sure this is your handiwork."

"Sounds like the words of a guilty man." Mike looked around the group of agents like he was looking for some sort of validation.

"That's the dumbest thing I've ever heard, Mike." He glanced to the agents standing around them. "What kind of motivation do we have to kill those guys?"

"It's no secret that you're trying to evict the family from your land." Mike sneered. "Sounds like one hell of a motivation to me. Not to mention Sabrina's hatred for me…she's been trying to make me look incompetent from the very beginning. She's been setting me up. I just couldn't believe it when I learned of her role in the shoot-out that took place with her fellow agents. I assume she must have thought she was shooting at me." He glared at her. "In case you were wondering, Agent Heath is still recovering at St. Pat's hospital."

He had been right. The people they'd been fighting on the mountain had been none other than the men from her own agency. But it didn't make sense. She should've known they were up there. Mike should have informed her that they might run into friendlies.

"Thanks to your mistakes, we have more than

enough evidence to take you and your whole family into custody." Mike gave him a weighted look, like he was sure he had the upper hand.

It took all of Trevor's strength not to get up in the man's face and tell him exactly where he could stuff his theories. In fact… He pushed his way toward the man and started screaming obscenities like some outraged hillbilly. While his mouth ran wild, he lifted Mike's gun from his holster and slipped it under his jacket.

"Trevor, stop!" Sabrina said. "Just go. Before you get into trouble. I'll get this figured out. I'm innocent. We both know that. We'll get this sorted."

He stepped beside her and gave her a long, passionate kiss. Their public display of affection caused some of the agents to look away. As they did, Sabrina slipped a gun into his waistband. She leaned in close like she was whispering something sweet into his ear, and said, "This is mine. Send it to ballistics along with the one from the cabin…and Mike's."

She must have seen him take the man's gun.

She moved back from their kiss. "Now get out of here before Mike does something stupid."

As far as Trevor was concerned, Mike had already done something extraordinarily idiotic when he decided to screw over Sabrina. And now his stupidity was going to come back to bite him. Trevor would not rest until he cleared the name of the woman he loved.

Chapter Fourteen

She was innocent, and he was the only person who could prove it.

From the truck, he watched as the agents paraded Sabrina into the building—like she was some kind of prized cattle that they just couldn't wait to take to slaughter. He would've thought that there would be more comradery within the FBI, but then it shouldn't come as such a surprise. It was a dog-eat-dog world.

Loyalty was a commodity in short supply.

Which made him think about Seattle. He couldn't be completely sure, but he had a feeling that the Bureau had taken the bait—if it hadn't, Mike would have certainly arrested him when they'd arrested Sabrina. As it was, they were probably still hoping to bring him down for gunrunning. He was probably still being watched.

If he caught a plane now, he could get to Seattle with a half a day to spare—hours in which he could put his plan into action.

His first stop was to the crime lab. When he arrived at the bland brick building he was reminded of a generic apartment building in New York—maybe in the low-rent district.

Chad was just parking when he arrived, and he parked beside him. As he got out Chad flashed him a little Ziploc bag; inside was a piece of shrapnel.

"What kind of mess have you gotten us into?" Chad asked.

"If I told you, you wouldn't believe me. But on a positive note, it looks like you and I will be flying to Seattle. We need to be there before the morning. In the mood for some spoon-melting coffee?" he asked with a chuckle.

Chad sighed and handed him the bag. "And here I thought moving to Montana would give us a chance to live a slower paced life. You just love proving me wrong, don't you?"

Trevor slapped his brother's arm. "It's not about proving you wrong, it's just about keeping the standard of living to which we've grown accustomed. I'd hate for you to get bored."

"I can't say life with you has ever been boring," Chad said with his trademark half grin.

"Good, then I'm not about to let you down." Trevor flashed his brother the two guns tucked into his waistband.

"Where did you get those?" Chad asked, giving him a look of concern.

"You're not gonna believe this, but I just lifted one off of one of our local FBI agents." Trevor smirked. "Best part, I doubt he even noticed it's missing."

"You have got to be kidding me," Chad said, each word like it was in independent sentence. "No wonder you have us running. We're going to be jumping borders in no time, aren't we?"

"It all depends on what happens in that building," he said, pointing toward the crime lab.

"Please tell me that there's a Get Out of Jail Free card somewhere in there." Chad frowned. "If I end up going to jail for you, I'm going to be irate."

He would have liked to tell his brother he had nothing to worry about, but the truth was that their butts were hanging way too far out in the open for him to feel comfortable. Mike, and the agents working with him, were going to be out for blood once they figured out what he had done.

"I'm going to run in. You need to call Zoey and have her arrange for a private jet to take us to Seattle. Got it?"

Chad nodded, already reaching for his phone.

As Trevor made his way into the crime lab, he looked back. Trish would've loved this kind of thing. She'd hated FBI agents even more than he did. Though now it seemed like he may well have fallen in love with one.

Trish would have given him such crap for Sabrina. But when push came to shove, his sister would have loved Sabrina just as much as he did. In fact, Trish would've probably helped him figure out a way to make everything work, not only with Sabrina but with this cluster he found them in.

He had no idea what he would do if this didn't work.

It wasn't just Sabrina's career that hung in the balance. If this failed, not only would he likely lose all credibility within the CIA and secret services, he'd also probably end up in jail, just as Chad had predicted. He would hate to prove his brother right.

In all of his years as a independent military contractor, he had never thought he would find himself in such a compromising position. He'd done many questionable things in the line of duty—but this was by far the craziest. It seemed like some kind of karmic slap that his greatest adversaries wouldn't be some terrorists abroad, but rather American law enforcement agents.

It didn't take long to hand the guns off to the tech at the lab; apparently Tina had already made the call.

When he made his way outside to Chad, his brother pointed toward his car and said, "Get in. We will have a jet waiting for you in the morning." Chad walked around to the driver's side.

Maybe this was all going to go better than he hoped, but he had a sinking feeling that he was in some deep water.

THE NEXT MORNING, the flight took just over an hour, and when they arrived Zoey was standing out on the tarmac waiting for them. Even in the overcast gray sky that seemed to always hover over the city, Zoey's black hair picked up what little light there was, and the effect created dark blue streaks. Even with her dyed locks, she looked so much like Trish.

There was a town car and a driver waiting beside her.

"Wipe that look off your face," Zoey said. "Stop worrying. I already hacked into the FBI mainframe. This Mike guy was bluffing, but he's hoping that they can bring you in for running guns. As such, I made sure he got orders from the top to intercept our 'trade' this evening. I also contacted the DOJ. they are sending someone to look into things and find out how deep this corruption runs."

"And what about Sabrina? Is she going to be cleared?" Trevor asked.

"Depends on her level of involvement. From what Chad was telling me, sounds like you and this woman have been hitting it off."

He shot a disapproving look at his brother, but Chad just shrugged.

"What can I say, man? We're a family that hates

to keep secrets from one another." Chad's half grin reappeared.

As ridiculous as his brother could be, he couldn't be mad at him. It was this open policy that was currently in the process of saving their butts.

"Sabrina and I have grown close since I got to the ranch," he admitted.

Zoey smiled. "Yeah, I knew she would be right up your alley when I vetted her for the housekeeping job."

"Oh yeah," Chad said. "I forgot that this was all your fault. Thanks a lot, sis. Maybe next time worry less about being our virtual matchmaker and worry more about whether or not the people we bring into our lives belong to the FBI."

Zoey held her hands up in surrender. "I admit, I may have overlooked the fact that her background seemed a bit sparse, but I just thought she was the kind of girl who didn't get out much."

"Well, you were definitely wrong." Trevor walked to the town car and threw their go bags into the trunk. "Then again, who am I to start pointing fingers? I assume Chad told you everything?"

Zoey nodded. "One thing for certain, you are gifted when it comes to getting us into highly unconventional situations."

That was one way to put it.

He once again thought of Trish. Zoey gave him

a mournful look. "Hey, Trevor, I know what you're thinking... It wasn't your fault."

He wasn't sure he believed her, or if he ever would.

"The family...we...none of us are upset with you about what happened back there. It was outside your control. You need to start forgiving yourself. Trish wouldn't want you to hang on to her death like you are."

It was easy enough for her to say, but she wasn't living in his shoes. "I hear what you're saying, but until we get through tonight unscathed, I'm not gonna forgive myself for anything."

Some tragedies were just too great to overcome... all he could do now was try not to repeat history.

Chapter Fifteen

Sabrina paced around the interrogation room. She couldn't even begin to count the number of times she had brought people in rooms like this one in order to get them to bend to her whims. And now here she was, on the other side of the table. There was a box of tissues and a stack of magazines at the center of the table. In the corner was a percolating coffeepot. The scent of coffee was there to promote a sense of safety, reminding people of being home and in the comfort of their own surroundings, but the aroma only made her more anxious.

At least they hadn't forced her to wear the cuffs around the building when they brought her up from her holding cell to the interrogation room this morning. It was already embarrassing enough that she had been brought in here like she was nothing more than one of their normal, run-of-the-mill murderers.

She was never going to be able to show her face around Missoula or the county again. Everyone in law enforcement knew, or had found out by now, that she had been arrested for murder. No doubt, they would have to call in an outside investigation team to review her case, but knowing Mike, he had gone out of his way to make sure she looked as guilty as hell.

What she couldn't understand was how. She'd had no intuition that they'd been watched or set up. Everything had seemed relatively...*normal*. Well, as normal as her days at the Bureau could be. Sure, not everybody came across dead bodies every few days, but in her line of work it was par for course.

Mike had to have been plotting this for some time—probably from the first moment they were sent to this remote agency from Washington.

She hadn't expected Mike to remain her friend, or even an ally, after they broke up. Things hadn't ended on the best of terms but they owed each other some amount of respect, especially after all they had been through. Instead here she was, standing on the other side of the glass thanks to his denigration of her character.

Even if she could prove her innocence, it would take some time. Certainly, the damage to her career would be nearly irreparable. Maybe she really would have to become a housekeeper. Maybe, just maybe, the Martins would hire her full time. But she had likely burned her bridge with that family, once the rest of Trevor's siblings found out about her role in the FBI.

As of the last she knew, Trevor had protected her secret, but now he'd have to out her in order to ask his family to help. Unfortunately. Even if his family did help, she wasn't sure that they would be her best allies when it came to standing in front of a judge and jury.

However, she could have sworn she'd heard Trevor say he was working with the CIA, but she couldn't believe it. If he had been working with the CIA like he said, there was no way that Mike would have sent her in to investigate the family. He had enough clearance to have that information.

But documents and proposals for the investigation had been fast-tracked through the Bureau. It was possible that either someone hadn't fact-checked properly or that Mike had known all along and had wanted her to disappear at the hands of the trained spook.

The CIA and their operatives, especially those who did not wish to be found, had been known to use their connections to make sure anyone who stepped in their way would fall prey to the shadowy nature of the agency.

There was a soft knock on the interrogation room door. "Yep," she said, awkwardly.

It didn't feel right to say anything at all, given the situation. But remaining silent also seemed equally odd. Speaking of remaining silent, she'd need to call in a lawyer.

"Good morning, Agent Parker," a female agent whom Sabrina didn't recognize said as she stepped into the room.

The woman had a pixie haircut that did nothing for the wrinkles that creased her forehead and were scattered around her eyes. Even her lips carried deep creases, like she spent one too many years smoking. As the woman walked into the interrogation room, Mike followed behind her, looking like a pit bull. He was out for blood, her blood, and seeing him made her skin prickle.

She wanted to go toe to toe with him and call him every obscenity that was rolling through her mind, but it would do no good. She couldn't deal with the situation proactively by being angry. All she could do was play his game—a game of logic and manipulation. Hopefully, she hadn't entered the game too late.

Actually, there was no time left for hope. She was already under arrest for crimes she hadn't committed. She'd already lost.

"I want my lawyer." The words tasted like the ocean, salty and smattered with the remnants of tempests.

"I bet you do," Mike said.

The woman gave him a look to shut up—it was the same look Sabrina had given him entirely too often when they were dating.

"Agent Parker, my name is Rowena Anderson. I'm the special agent in charge from your sister agency, the Madison County resident office," the woman said, an air of authority in her tone.

"Pleasure," Sabrina said, unsure whether or not she should play nice or say nothing. It didn't seem as though it would be in her best interest to be an ass.

"Yes," the woman said. "I hope you slept well. I'm sorry it took me so long to get here."

She hadn't slept a wink. Instead she had spent the entire night staring up at the ceiling of her cell and thinking about all the ways her life had gone wrong. For both their sakes, she said nothing.

Agent Anderson pointed toward the chair beside the table and motioned for her to sit down.

She did as instructed, but she couldn't take her eyes off Mike's smug face. Looking at him, and the way he seemed to have no remorse for what he had done to her, she couldn't understand what she had ever seen in him. He was nothing but a weasel.

"Agent Parker, it is with my deepest regrets that we have to meet under such circumstances. However, I'm sure that you understand, thanks to your many years of dedicated service for the FBI, that we all must do our duty. Today, my duty is to talk to you about your role in the two deaths that occurred while you were representing the Bureau undercover." The woman walked over to the coffeepot and poured herself a cup. "Would you like some?"

The woman was stalling—it was a common interrogation technique. It was the same reason they had kept her locked up in this room for four hours before anyone had even acknowledged her presence. They wanted to make her nervous, to drive up her anxiety level to the point where she'd be easier to manipulate.

By the same token, Agent Anderson had to know that Sabrina was fully aware of her tactics.

The woman took a long sip of her coffee, staring at her through the steam—she was trying to get a read on her. No doubt, she wanted to feel her out in order to determine how she would play this interrogation.

"Sabrina, it's in your best interest to just admit you killed those two Cussler guys. We found your fingerprints all over the murder weapon." Mike smirked.

Oh, that bastard.

It was a good thing she had sat down. Her hands fell limp into her lap as the shock worked its way through her body.

Her fingerprints had been found on the murder weapon?

It was impossible.

She'd never even fired her gun—only the one that Trevor had given her on the mountain, a gun she had returned to him. Her own firearm she'd given to Trevor, so Mike couldn't have sent it off to the lab for analysis. This didn't make sense.

She wanted to cry out and to tell Agent Anderson that she had no idea what he was talking about.

But she knew that they must have had concrete evidence well in advance of her arrest. Which meant they had a different gun...a gun she had likely never actually touched.

At the shanty, she had watched Trevor pick up the gun that had killed the first brother. He'd wiped it down and left it there. She'd never touched it—or even gone back inside the shack. But that didn't mean someone hadn't tampered with the evidence. If the FBI, or Mike, had gone to that shanty they easily could have planted her prints on that gun. Or maybe there was an entirely different gun. She just couldn't be sure.

If only they had just called in Wyatt and the sheriff's department when they found the body. Wyatt was probably going to have a fit when he learned where she was. If he admitted to his role in her supposed cover-up of the second Cussler brother's death, his future would be in jeopardy. Everything she had done, every choice she had made, had been wrong.

"Nothing to say for yourself?" Mike said, taunting her.

"Agent Couer, I told you that if you wished to stand in on this interrogation, you were to remain silent," the woman said. "As you seem incapable of such a daunting task, and given your familiarity with Agent Parker, I think it best that you leave." She pointed toward the door.

Mike opened his mouth to argue, but quickly shut up. It was the smartest thing she'd ever seen him do.

If only she could tell the woman the truth. And yet this woman had no reason to believe anything she said. It was normal for the accused to immediately start blaming others. A perpetrator rarely admitted fault. And even if they did passively admit to some wrongdoing, there would always be some extenuating circumstance that explained their misdeed away. She couldn't be like one of those people. But she also couldn't sit here and be accused and do nothing.

Mike stepped out of the room, but not before giving her one last sidelong glance and an accompanying smirk. The door clicked shut behind him.

"Now, Agent Parker, back to our conversation," the woman said.

"I didn't kill anyone. I'm innocent." She put her hands on the table, palms up, the universal sign of submission and forthrightness.

The woman looked down at Sabrina's hands and then in the direction of the closed door. "I have reviewed the entire case, and the evidence they have against you. As of this moment, the evidence is not in your favor. However, I'm finding holes in Agent Couer's assessment of the situation."

Sabrina wasn't entirely sure what the woman meant, so she remained silent.

"There's not a lot of information I can give you at this time. However, if you help me in my investigation, it will not go unnoticed."

She implied she would get Sabrina a deal without directly offering anything. When interrogating, Sabrina used the same method to elicit trust from her suspects.

She couldn't get sucked into this woman's charade.

"And what is it that you would like me to do?" Sabrina asked, curious.

Agent Anderson looked back at the door, almost as though she expected it to open again at any second. If anything, it appeared as if she were more nervous than Sabrina was. "About the meeting in Seattle. We want you there. Along with Agent Couer."

"What? Why?" Did they want to publicly broadcast her shame for the rest of the Bureau? No. She wasn't going to be their whipping boy.

"I know you're gun-shy after what happened. But believe me when I say it's in your best interest to help me out." The woman reached over and gave Sabrina's hand a reassuring squeeze.

The simple action surprised her. The interrogation room was currently being filmed. Was the woman trying to tell her something that she couldn't say on camera? Or was she stringing her along?

"Trevor said he worked for the CIA. You don't think he's really involved with the illegal gun trade, do you?"

"Oh, he and his family are very involved," Agent Anderson said. "We believe he may be using it to increase his income. It's fairly common for those behind the curtain to participate in unsanctioned deals like this."

Sabrina couldn't help but feel even more deflated. The man she had fallen in love with couldn't be a criminal. He wasn't the man the Bureau made him out to be.

If they went to Seattle, she risked being made an even a bigger fool in the Bureau, and yet she would get to see Trevor at least one more time. And she could prove that she had been right about distrusting him.

For all she knew, he wouldn't even be there and instead it would be a team of his people. It would be smart of him to call off the entire deal now that he knew that he and his family were under investigation by the Bureau.

A part of her also wanted to save him. If she went there, she could try to alert him to the danger.

She was already damned by the Bureau's standards, and probably out of a job now that she was under arrest. Even though she was innocent, she would be lucky if she didn't go to prison.

A chill ran down her spine as she thought about being stuck in a federal prison with inmates she had sent there. The situation wouldn't end well— but from the beginning of her investigation, the only thing that had gone well was the night she spent in the mountains with Trevor making love.

If only she could go back in time…to a time and place where things weren't so complicated.

Chapter Sixteen

The gun sat heavy in Trevor's hands. Though the assault rifle weighed only a few pounds, it felt as though it was imbued with the weight of everyone who depended on him.

Zoey was sitting in the corner office, out of sight from where their operation would take place. Even if he couldn't get out, perhaps she would.

Though they had planned everything to the last detail, it didn't mean that it would go off without a hitch. Things had a way of going haywire any time guns were involved. He would be lucky if he made it out alive.

Chad was sitting above him in the skywalk, and as Trevor looked up, his brother gave him a thumbs-up. In a matter of seconds, and with a rearrangement of fabric, Chad disappeared into the darkness, perfectly camouflaged. For all intents and purposes, Trevor appeared to be alone.

In the quiet of the industrial warehouse, the buzz

of the fluorescent lights sounded like a swarm of bees just waiting to descend.

Between the FBI and a swarm of bees, under normal circumstances, he would take bees.

He hated that this was where they were now—playing a game of corrupt politics and misguided leadership.

Though it appeared he was standing alone in the center of the industrial building, he could feel people watching him. No doubt, by now they likely had agents set up around the building monitoring him with some hidden tech. They likely had microphones and video cameras installed in the building as soon as they heard of their plan—if they were smart, they had every inch of this place streaming live at some central command center.

His phone pinged. It was time. Everything was in place.

The metal industrial garage door clicked as someone slid it open. In front of him was Gus, the man they had hired to help flush out Mike. Gus had been working for them over the last decade, always available at a moment's notice. They paid him well, but this time he wasn't sure if they were paying the man enough to deal with what was about to happen.

This time, Gus had brought three men and a woman with him. Gus was wearing a tailored linen suit, and his gray hair was slicked back with pomade. He reminded Trevor of a Miami drug lord.

The men and women standing guard around Gus all wore black, and each had a pair of Ray-Ban sunglasses perched on their head—and they looked terribly out of place in Seattle's underbelly.

He gave the man a stiff nod. "Did Ahmal send you?"

"Does Ahmal send just anyone?" Gus said, looking at him like he was a stranger he didn't trust.

He played his role well.

"You have what I asked for?" Gus asked, motioning toward the big rig that was parked by the far wall of the warehouse.

"You have our money?" Trevor asked, lowering the assault rifle in his hand and leaning on it as if it were nothing more than a walking stick.

Gus looked toward the gun at Trevor's side. "Is that one of our M16s?"

Trevor took a step forward, moving to hand the man the gun. The woman stepped between them, as though she was really there to guard the man his family had planted.

Perfect.

"Have your woman stand down," he said, glaring at her.

"Marie," Gus said, sounding tired.

The woman stepped back, but her hand had moved to the gun strapped to her side.

Hopefully, Gus had told her that this mission was nothing more than a farce. He didn't want to have to worry about drawing any unnecessary friendly fire—he had enough to worry about when it came to the FBI and what they did or didn't know. One wrong move, one misplaced statement, and all hell could rain down.

He handed Gus the gun, keeping one eye on the woman to make sure she didn't make a mistake. Gus was smart, but just like them, he probably wanted to make this seem as real as possible—which may have meant that he had left his team in the dark.

"There are a thousand more of these inside that truck." He motioned behind him. "Did you wire us the money?"

"I only work in cash. I find it comforting," Gus said, motioning for one of his guards.

As the guard stepped forward, Trevor noticed the black briefcase in his hand. The briefcase was leather and adorned with brass, perfectly antiquated. It was almost comical, and far from the kind of thing most people would've expected, but Trevor had seen a lot of eccentricity in his travels.

In fact, one of the warlords they had been investigating in Africa brought a capuchin monkey to all their arms deals. In the end, STEALTH had planted a recording device in the monkey's collar. Because of a pet monkey, a dangerous man had been brought to justice and found guilty of war crimes.

"Half a million?" Trevor asked, reaching in his pocket and taking out the keys to the truck.

"In unmarked bills," Gus said. "Show us the guns."

Trevor walked toward the truck. Each step felt like it was in slow motion, as though he were walking toward his execution.

If this was how he went down… No, he couldn't give it any thought.

Trish, and the last look on her face—the look of terror, pain and the realization that death was upon her—came to the front of his mind and a wave of nausea threatened to take him to his knees. Somehow he kept walking.

The end of the truck was open, exposing the crates. Stepping up, Gus followed him and he reached inside the open crate nearest them. The guns had been chipped, even though this wasn't that kind of deal. Everything reminded him of the last time. He'd promised himself he would never be in this kind of situation again, and as he moved toward the crate his body stopped. It was as though he was glued to the floor of the truck, and no matter how badly he wanted to step forward and look inside that crate, his body wouldn't allow it.

"You like?" Trevor asked, trying to ignore the way his body defied him.

"They are all identical?" Gus asked.

Trevor nodded. They stepped out of the truck and Gus's men closed the back end.

The guard handed Gus the briefcase.

"Do we have a deal?" Trevor asked.

Gus handed him the briefcase and Trevor handed him the keys to the big rig. Every door in the warehouse flew open. There was the percussion of a flash bang, and Trevor hit the ground.

"Get down on the ground!" a man ordered. "Hands above your head!"

The FBI agents rushed into the building, running through the smoke of the blast. Trevor watched as Mike ran toward him, his gun raised. Sabrina was nowhere in sight.

Was she in danger? He had been assured by his people at the CIA that they had spoken to the folks at the Bureau and cleared everything up. But had there been more mistakes? Had the FBI screwed up again? Or had he been set up?

Mike glanced around, making sure that he was covered by the smoke and no one was close as he stopped beside Trevor. "Stand up, jackass," he ordered.

Trevor moved to his feet as he reached for his gun.

"Oh, please do… I've been looking forward to killing you." Mike's finger tightened on the trigger of the gun that was pointed straight at Trevor's chest.

"Mike, stop! Don't shoot!" he yelled, hoping that he could alert the FBI agents around him before this thing went all kinds of sideways and they ended up in a total firefight.

A shot rang out, rising above the melee of sounds

around them of men and women shouting. Everything stopped.

Instinctively, Trevor pulled his gun as he did a mental check of his body. Nothing hurt, but adrenaline had a funny way of masking pain and he couldn't risk looking down to check himself for bullet holes.

Sabrina and another female agent stepped through the smoke behind Mike, each with their weapon raised. Trevor dropped his weapon and lifted his hands. Mike lowered his arms and there was a look of shock on his face.

"What in the hell?" Mike said, turning toward the women.

Blood seeped from his back, glossy and wet against the black fabric of his suit jacket.

"Get on the ground!" the other agent with Sabrina ordered.

"But—" Mike started.

"I said, get on the ground!" the woman repeated.

Instead of following orders, Mike raised the gun, pointing it straight at Sabrina. As he moved, Trevor lunged toward the man. He couldn't hurt her. Not Sabrina. Not this time.

There was the crunching sound of bones breaking as Mike's body hit the ground beneath him.

Grabbing the gun in Mike's hand, he flipped it out of his grip and threw it to the side.

He pulled the man's arms behind his bleeding back. "Mike Couer, you are under arrest for the murder of Owen and Earl Cussler, tampering with evidence, corruption, and impeding a federal investigation. Anything you say can and will be used against you in a court of law."

The agent beside Sabrina stepped beside them and Mirandized him.

Watching Sabrina stand over Mike with her gun drawn was a thing of beauty. This time, evil didn't win.

Chapter Seventeen

The private jet was full of Trevor's family, friends and a few of the agents from the case; yet as Sabrina sat there beside Trevor, it was as if they were all alone. This wasn't how she had expected things to go. Nothing could have prepared her for the things that Rowena had told her on their way to Seattle. She had described her plan to take down of one of the most corrupt officials in the Pacific Northwest, and explained how Sabrina could help.

Mike had been transported to Seattle's Harborview Medical Center and would remain under surveillance until he was completely out of the woods from his gunshot wound. Admittedly, it had felt good to shoot the man who had threatened to take Trevor down.

She reached over and took Trevor's hand.

He looked at her. "You okay?"

Though it had only been a day, it felt as though months had passed, thanks to all the statements she'd been required to give and all the legal paperwork that needed to be completed. Rowena had been diligent in making sure that everything was filed and completed in a way that would leave Sabrina free and clear and able to jump right back into her position at the FBI when she was ready.

For the time being, she wasn't sure what she wanted to do. She definitely needed a break from things to assess her future.

"Babe? Do you need anything?" Trevor asked, pulling her from her thoughts.

"Oh no, I'm okay." Her voice sounded tired. She wasn't sure he was ready to give her what she needed now.

"It's going to be okay," he said, giving her a kiss on the forehead.

Undoubtedly, the Martins would want to leave Montana now that their quiet retirement had been upended…a situation that she herself had a role in creating. If only she had seen Mike for the man he had truly been when they were together.

As it turned out, their relationship had not only been terrible, it had been a sham from the very beginning. Mike had been using her to learn about his enemies all while sending her into this and other investigations half-cocked with spotty information—in the end, no doubt hoping to humiliate her. If only she'd realized what he was doing, smearing her name and thereby delegitimizing anything she might say about him or his dealings. She felt so used...and so angry.

But Mike would pay for his full-blown assault on her character. And she would happily take the stand should she need to.

Trevor's phone buzzed. Opening up his email, he smiled.

"What is it?" she asked.

"Ballistics came in on your gun and Mike's." He moved the screen so she could see the message. "The slug they pulled from Earl was fired from Mike's gun...not the one they found at the shack, or yours."

Rowena leaned forward from the seat behind them and tapped her on the shoulder. "It looks like we just got a little more good news."

"What do you mean?" Trevor asked.

"In addition to your ballistics, the Evidence Response Team found the hunting cabin Sabrina told me you had been looking for." Rowena showed her a photo on her phone of a graying log cabin almost completely shrouded within a thicket of barberry. "About five hundred yards from the cabin, the ERT located a shallow mass grave. It appears to contain the remains of three men—one older, who we believe may have been the father—and two women. Right now, we can't confirm or deny their identities, but it appears that they are the rest of the Cusslers. My team is looking for the other family that was reportedly in the area, but so far they haven't found anything to indicate their whereabouts."

"Do you know what happened to the Cusslers? How they died?" Sabrina asked.

"It looks like it was execution style—but one had taken a shot to the kidney shortly before the time of death. They are guessing the guy was shot in the back—probably running. There was some level of healing, which means he may have been held for a day or two before he was executed." Rowena's lips puckered.

"How long had they been dead?" Sabrina asked, thinking back to the blood she had first found behind the shanty.

"They'd been down for a few days to a week at least."

"They are going to pull DNA and confirm identities as well as run any lead they recover through ballistics," Rowena continued. "I'd bet dollars to doughnuts that they were fired from Agent Couer's gun."

"How is the man I shot… Agent Heath?" Sabrina asked.

"It looks like he took a hit up there on that mountain, as Mike said. And while Agent Heath may have been acting on Agent Couer's orders, he also may have had a role in setting you up. We believe it was their plan to pick a time and place when there were no other witnesses—but then things went haywire."

"We got lucky."

"Not entirely. We have reason to believe he retrieved the gun from the Cussler shack and planted it in your things at your house at the Martins'. Needless to say, whether or not you were the one who pulled the trigger, it was a job well done." Rowena winked at her. "He is going to be thoroughly questioned, but I have a feeling he, too, will be spending quite a while in prison."

Sabrina smiled. She'd had a soft spot for Agent Heath, but if he had anything to do with trying to take her down, she'd be fine never hearing the man's name again. "Rowena, thanks for everything. I would have gone down for this if you hadn't started digging. I appreciate it."

The woman gave a humble nod. "It's my job. And if someone tried to do this kind of thing to me, I would expect my fellow agents to see it to the end as well. Besides, we women of the Bureau have to stick together."

She wasn't kidding.

Rowena started to sit back in her seat but stopped. "Oh, and hey, I got word that there is going to be an open seat at the Missoula office…you wouldn't be interested in being the special agent in charge, would you?" Rowena said, cracking an elusive smile.

Trevor looked over at her and gave her a proud, approving grin.

What she really wanted to do was stay with him.

On the other hand, her job was her life. Though her office would only be a short drive away, long hours and the stress that came with her job would inevitably drive a wedge between them. She was cut from the FBI cloth, and no matter what happened in her life, she didn't want to lose who she was.

"I'd love to take the job…you know, *if* it were to come my way," she said.

Rowena winked and sat back, taking her phone out and clicking on email. "I'll see what I can do for you."

Sabrina turned to Trevor.

"Way to go," Trevor said, but some of the light in his eyes had seemed to fade as he too must have realized what her job would do to their relationship.

"Thank you," she said, lowering her head so she could whisper to him alone. "But the truth is… I don't know if it's going to work."

"Why not?" He frowned.

She had always been told that a woman should never say *I love you* first, but she'd never been very good at being told what to do.

"Trevor, here's the deal… I love you. I know that what we had…it was probably just a forced proximity thing that was kind of convenient, but—"

"Our relationship was not *convenient*," he said, interrupting her. "I'm not the kind of guy who takes a woman to bed just for the hell of it."

"Oh yeah?" she asked, giving him a playful look. "Then you do it just for the jollies?"

He smirked. "No. I took you to bed because the second I saw you standing outside the shack that first day, I knew you were something—*someone*— special." He lifted their entwined hands and gave her fingers a soft kiss. "I loved you before we even met... I know it sounds crazy, but it was like we were made for each other...as if cosmic forces brought us together. I mean, think of the odds that were stacked against us ever even meeting, and then there we were at the same time and the same place, fighting the same side of a battle that we didn't even know we were fighting." His face flushed. "I sound ridiculous."

"No, you're cute when you're flustered," she said, happiness racing through her. "I didn't know you had it in you."

"Hey now," he said with a laugh. "If you're going to tease me, I don't have to keep going."

"No," she said, motioning for him to continue. "I like seeing you act the way I feel."

"Wait..." he started. "You didn't forget we had a bet riding on all this, did you? Turns out I was completely right about you being the target."

"Oh, yeah," she said, staring at him as they whisked through the clouds. The heat in her cheeks rose as she remembered the stakes. "Who do you think you are, Mr. Martin? Do you think you can really use a bet to get me back into bed?"

"First, I'm the man who is going to love you for the rest of our lives. And second, I would never make you do anything you didn't want to do."

"Well, we did strike a deal," she teased, giving him an impish look.

"That's what I like to hear. I can't wait to get home," he said, laughing. "By the way, what was the favor you were going to ask for if you won?"

When they made the bet, she hadn't had a clue. Everything between them had been so distorted that she hadn't even really believed that they would get to the bottom of their investigation in time for her to save her job, let alone see who won the bet. Yet here and now, she knew exactly what she should have wished for.

"Are you sure you want to hear it?"

Trevor nodded.

"If I'd won, I'd have asked you to marry me." She gazed into his eyes, half expecting him to choke and shirk away, but instead he leaned in closer so their foreheads touched. "You're right, it's like we are meant to be together. When I look at you, I see a father to my children, a husband, a friend. When we are close all I want to do is move even closer. And when I was arrested, all I wanted was to know that you were safe and taken care of." She paused. "I know my asking you isn't conventional, but I can't stand the thought of losing you. Will you?"

"Baby, nothing about us has been conventional. I'd hate for us to start now." He smiled a smile larger than any she had seen. "I'd marry you right now if we could. So, yes. Absolutely." He reached up and took her chin between his thumb and forefinger. "I love you, Sabrina Parker. And I always will."

"And I you, Trevor Martin."

He leaned in to kiss her, but she stopped him. "And one more thing," she said with a grin.

"What?" he asked, his eyes heavy with lust.

"I'm keeping Cap'n Crunch around in case this thing goes south."

"Anything for you."

She giggled as their lips met. He tasted of promises, the savories of a life filled with adventure, and the sweetness of forever.

* * * * *

Look for the next book in the STEALTH series,
In His Sights,
available January 2020
wherever Harlequin Intrigue books
and ebooks are sold.

WE HOPE YOU ENJOYED THIS BOOK!

INTRIGUE

Dive into action-packed suspense.
Solve crimes. Pursue justice.

Look for six new books available every
month, wherever books are sold!

Harlequin.com

SAFETY BREACH
Longview Ridge Ranch • by Delores Fossen

Former profiler Gemma Hanson is in witness protection, but she's still haunted by memories of the serial killer who tried to kill her last year. Her concerns skyrocket when Sheriff Kellan Slater tells her the murderer has learned her location and is coming to finish what he started.

UNDERCOVER ACCOMPLICE
Red, White and Built: Delta Force Deliverance
by Carol Ericson

When Delta Force soldier Hunter Mancini learns the group that kidnapped CIA operative Sue Chandler is now framing his team leader, he asks for her help. But could she be hiding something that would clear his boss?

AMBUSHED AT CHRISTMAS
Rushing Creek Crime Spree • by Barb Han

After a jogger resembling Detective Leah Cordon is murdered, rancher Deacon Kent approaches her, believing the attack is related to recent cattle mutilations. Can they find the killer before he corners Leah?

DANGEROUS CONDITIONS
Protectors at Heart • by Jenna Kernan

Former soldier Logan Lynch's first investigation as the constable of a small town leads him to microbiologist Paige Morris, whose boss was killed. Yet as they search for the murderer, Paige is forced to reveal a secret that shows the stakes couldn't be higher.

RULES IN DEFIANCE
Blackhawk Security • by Nichole Severn

Blackhawk Security investigator Elliot Dunham never expected his neighbor to show up bruised and covered in blood in the middle of the night. To protect Waylynn Hargraves, Elliot must defy the rules he's set for himself, because he knows he's all that stands between her and certain death.

HIDDEN TRUTH
Stealth • by Danica Winters

When undercover CIA agent Trevor Martin meets Sabrina Parker, the housekeeper at the ranch where he's lying low, he doesn't know she's an undercover FBI agent. After a murder on the property, the operatives must work together, but can they discover their hidden connection before it's too late?

HIATMBPA1219

INTRIGUE

Available December 17, 2019

HICNM1219

"Who's in the house?" he asked.

Another head shake from Laney. "A man. I didn't see his face."

Not that he needed it, but Owen had more confirmation of the danger. He saw that Laney had a gun, a small snub-nosed .38. It didn't belong to him, nor was it one that he'd ever seen in the guesthouse where Laney was staying. Later, he'd ask her about it, about why she hadn't mentioned that she had a weapon, but for now they obviously had a much bigger problem.

Owen texted his brother again, to warn him about the intruder so that Kellan didn't walk into a situation that could turn deadly. He also asked Kellan to call in more backup. If the person upstairs started shooting, Owen wanted all the help he could get.

"What happened?" Owen whispered to Laney.

She opened her mouth, paused and then closed it as if she'd changed her mind about what to say. "About ten minutes ago, I was in the kitchen with Addie when the power went off. A few seconds later, a man came in through the front door and I hid in the pantry with her until he went upstairs."

Smart thinking on Laney's part to hide instead of panicking or confronting the guy. But it gave Owen an uneasy feeling that Laney could think that fast under such pressure. And then there was the gun again. Where had she got it? The guesthouse was on the other side of the backyard, much farther away than the barn. If she'd gone to the guesthouse to get the gun, why hadn't she just stayed there with Addie? It would have been safer than running across the yard with the baby.

"Did you get a good look at the man?" Owen prompted.

Laney again shook her head. "But I heard him. When he stepped into the house, I knew it wasn't you, so I guessed it must be trouble."

Again, quick thinking on her part. He wasn't sure why, though, that gave him a very uneasy feeling.

"I didn't hear or see a vehicle," Laney added.

Owen hadn't seen one, either, which meant the guy must have come on foot. Not impossible, but Owen's ranch was a good half mile from the main road. If this was a thief, he wasn't going to get away with much. Plus, it would be damn brazen of some idiot to break into a cop's home just to commit a robbery.

So what was really going on?

Don't miss
A Threat to His Family *by Delores Fossen,*
available January 2020 wherever
Harlequin® Intrigue books and ebooks are sold.

www.Harlequin.com

Don't miss this holiday Western romance from *USA TODAY* bestselling author

DELORES FOSSEN

Sometimes a little Christmas magic can rekindle the most unexpected romances...

"Fossen creates sexy cowboys and fast-moving plots that will take your breath away." —Lori Wilde, *New York Times* bestselling author

Order your copy today!

HQNBooks.com

PHDFCWC1119

Get 4 FREE REWARDS!

We'll send you 2 FREE Books plus <u>2</u> FREE Mystery Gifts.

Harlequin Intrigue® books feature heroes and heroines that confront and survive danger while finding themselves irresistibly drawn to one another.

FREE Value Over $20

YES! Please send me 2 FREE Harlequin Intrigue® novels and my 2 FREE gifts (gifts are worth about $10 retail). After receiving them, if I don't wish to receive any more books, I can return the shipping statement marked "cancel." If I don't cancel, I will receive 6 brand-new novels every month and be billed just $4.99 each for the regular-print edition or $5.99 each for the larger-print edition in the U.S., or $5.74 each for the regular-print edition or $6.49 each for the larger-print edition in Canada. That's a savings of at least 12% off the cover price! It's quite a bargain! Shipping and handling is just 50¢ per book in the U.S. and $1.25 per book in Canada.* I understand that accepting the 2 free books and gifts places me under no obligation to buy anything. I can always return a shipment and cancel at any time. The free books and gifts are mine to keep no matter what I decide.

Choose one: ☐ **Harlequin Intrigue®**
Regular-Print
(182/382 HDN GNXC)

☐ **Harlequin Intrigue®**
Larger-Print
(199/399 HDN GNXC)

Name (please print)

Address   Apt. #

City   State/Province   Zip/Postal Code

Mail to the **Reader Service:**
IN U.S.A.: P.O. Box 1341, Buffalo, NY 14240-8531
IN CANADA: P.O. Box 603, Fort Erie, Ontario L2A 5X3

Want to try 2 free books from another series? Call 1-800-873-8635 or visit www.ReaderService.com.

---

*Terms and prices subject to change without notice. Prices do not include sales taxes, which will be charged (if applicable) based on your state or country of residence. Canadian residents will be charged applicable taxes. Offer not valid in Quebec. This offer is limited to one order per household. Books received may not be as shown. Not valid for current subscribers to Harlequin Intrigue books. All orders subject to approval. Credit or debit balances in a customer's account(s) may be offset by any other outstanding balance owed by or to the customer. Please allow 4 to 6 weeks for delivery. Offer available while quantities last.

Your Privacy—The Reader Service is committed to protecting your privacy. Our Privacy Policy is available online at www.ReaderService.com or upon request from the Reader Service. We make a portion of our mailing list available to reputable third parties that offer products we believe may interest you. If you prefer that we not exchange your name with third parties, or if you wish to clarify or modify your communication preferences, please visit us at www.ReaderService.com/consumerschoice or write to us at Reader Service Preference Service, P.O. Box 9062, Buffalo, NY 14240-9062. Include your complete name and address.

HI20

Love Harlequin romance?

DISCOVER.

Be the first to find out about promotions,
news and exclusive content!

 Facebook.com/HarlequinBooks

 Twitter.com/HarlequinBooks

 Instagram.com/HarlequinBooks

 Pinterest.com/HarlequinBooks

ReaderService.com

EXPLORE.

Sign up for the Harlequin e-newsletter and
download a free book from any series at
TryHarlequin.com.

CONNECT.

Join our Harlequin community to share
your thoughts and connect with other
romance readers!
Facebook.com/groups/HarlequinConnection

HARLEQUIN®

**ROMANCE WHEN
YOU NEED IT**

HSOCIAL2018